Exposed:

When Good Wives Go Bad

Exposed:

When Good Wives Go Bad

Anna J.

www.urbanbooks.net

Urban Books, LLC
97 N18th Street
Wyandanch, NY 11798

Exposed: When Good Wives Go Bad Copyright © 2013
Anna J.

ISBN 13: 978-1-60162-562-5
ISBN 10: 1-60162-562-6

First Printing October 2013
Printed in the United States of America

10 9 8 7 6 5 4 3 2 1

*This is a work of fiction. Any references or similarities
to actual events, real people, living or dead, or to real
locales are intended to give the novel a sense of reality.
Any similarity in other names, characters, places, and
incidents is entirely coincidental.*

Distributed by Kensington Publishing Corp.
Submit Wholesale Orders to:
Kensington Publishing Corp.
C/O Penguin Group (USA) Inc.
Attention: Order Processing
405 Murray Hill Parkway
East Rutherford, NJ 07073-2316
Phone: 1-800-526-0275
Fax: 1-800-227-9604

Also By Anna J

Novels

My Woman His Wife 3: Playing for Keeps
Hell's Diva 2: Mecca's Return
Hell's Diva: Mecca's Mission
Snow White: A Survival Story
My Little Secret
Get Money Chicks
The Aftermath
My Woman His Wife

Anthologies

Full Figured 4
Bedroom Chronicles
The Cat House
Flexin' and Sexin': Sexy Street Tales Vol 1
Fantasy
Fetish
Morning Noon and Night: Can't Get Enough
Stories To Excite You: Ménage Quad

Independent Projects

Lies Told In the Bedroom
Motives 1&2
Erotic Snapshots Volumes 1-6

For every woman who has ever had to deal with a situation that was out of her control . . . this one is for you!

Dear Reader,

In writing this book, I know for certain that the stories that I am telling will hit home for a lot of you. Although this is a fictional read, domestic violence is a serious situation that happens more often than reported. Both women and men are subjected to domestic abuse whether it be physical, verbal, or mental. None of which should be taken lightly. Having been in an abusive situation at a point in my life, I never thought that today I would be able to tell the story and give insight for those who are still trapped in it. If you or you know someone who is in an abusive relationship don't give up on them . . . even if they keep going back. It's a cycle that only those who have ever been in an abusive situation can understand. Especially if you are a woman. We are always trying to be superheroes and we always think that we can save and help everyone. Thankfully I was able to get away from my situation, and I now know my worth so I have never gone back into one. It doesn't always work that way for everyone. So practice patience with those that you know may be hurting, and although it's hard and frustrating *don't give up on them!*

If this is your first time reading one of my novels you have a lot of catching up to do! Thank you for your support, and for all of you who have been riding with me since *My Woman His Wife* I truly appreciate the love. I am so thankful to be living all of my dreams, and I love that I have faithful fans who are staying on with me through it all. As with any dream, there is a team behind

Dear Reader

me and God has put so many people in my life that it's unbelievable at times. Chereme Sanders, you walked with me through the entire process of writing this book. Thank you for your honesty, and for giving me the voice of an avid reader. Not every writer is blessed to have that kind of support, and someone to tell them that something isn't sounding right! Thanks for that, and thanks for being a true friend. Love ya!

Debra Brown aka DB! Thanks for being my number one fan. You know I got two copies on deck for you and your daughter, so you won't have to yell at me this time. Thanks for the support on every book, whether it's a novel or an e-read. You are one of the fans who always buy the book twice! One for your bookshelf and one for your Kindle. Thanks for everything babe. Love you to pieces!

To all of my friends, family, FB peeps, and IG lovies, thank you all for your support, and for your reviews! You know we need those as authors. This book was more personal for me than my others. Just as personal as *Snow White* was when I wrote that book. Every time I give you a novel it's from experience although the story is fabricated. I appreciate each and every one of you, and I look forward to hearing your reviews on this one. As always, enjoy the ride and be sure to spread the word!

Aspiring authors take hold of your title. Either you are an author or you're not. I don't aspire to be great, I already am. I merely work at polishing my craft so that I can become better at it. I've never considered myself an aspiring anything. Even before I wrote my first book I told people *I am a writer*. If you keep aspiring to do something you may never get it done. If you are something, you will perfect it. Claim it! Own it!

~Anna J

Part One

Darius and Simone

—Janet Jackson, "What About"

1

Eye Opener

Does he threaten to hurt you, your kids, or a family pet? Does he make you ask for money? Does he threaten to harm himself if you try to leave? Does he make you stay in the house until he gets home? Does he treat you like a child?

"Bitch, why do you make me act like this? Why do you always have to do something stupid?" My rage-filled husband showered questions down on me one behind the other, but I was unable to answer him.

Whap! A closed fist connected with my right eye, making me see stars. This had been going on for what felt like the past twenty minutes, and I just wanted it to stop. I wasn't even sure what I did this time, and I couldn't curl up any tighter in this corner than I already was. My nose was bleeding from the impact of him slamming my face into the wall moments earlier, and a patch of my hair was lying next to me on the floor.

Does he go into drunken fits? Does he blame you for his indiscretions? Does he promise to stop the violence only to do it again? Does he beat you in front of your children? Is he different around family members?

"How many times do I have to tell you that I run this shit? This is my muthafuckin' castle! I only allow you to live because I'm a nice person. . . ."

Crack! A size thirteen Timberland boot came crashing down on my rib cage; the pain was unbearable. He rained blows down on me like I was a stranger . . . like we hadn't spent most of our lives together. The room was getting black, and I was almost certain I was on my way out of here. *If I can just get to my pocketbook I can fix this. . . .*

Does he hold you hostage? Does he threaten to end his life? Does he promise to get help? Does he abuse you then want to have sex? Does he make you look like you're the one with the problem? We'll keep asking until the violence stops. . . .

"You better not die on me, bitch, you hear me? I'm sorry I had to do this to you. You just get me so jealous sometimes. Come on, baby. Let me help you up."

As I struggled to get up from the floor I saw the remnants of what used to be an abuse hotline packet. A nurse slipped it to me while I was in the emergency room a few weeks ago trying to explain how I broke my arm. Being a Philadelphia police officer gave me an excuse as to what happened, but the nurse wasn't buying what my husband was trying to sell her. When she asked me what happened I opened my mouth to tell her the lie I already had formulated in my head, hoping it wasn't one I had already used, but my husband of ten long years spoke before I did.

"She doesn't speak English."

Of course the nurse looked at me like she didn't believe him, but I was wise enough to keep my damn mouth shut. Hell, keeping my mouth shut would have been wiser to do an hour before and maybe my ass wouldn't have ended up in the emergency room of the University of Pennsylvania hospital at three in the damn morning when I had to get up for work in a few hours. I guessed I'd be using another one of those sick days the police force was kind enough to give me.

I wasn't really sure when it all began, but tonight like so many other nights felt like déjà vu. I thought everything was going well. We were at a mutual friend's house celebrating four years of marriage and a newborn child. I found myself gazing at the child absently, rubbing my hand across my stomach. Darius and I tried four times to conceive, and each time it ended in a miscarriage.

My doctor said that my stress level was way too high to carry a child, and that was part of the reason why my pregnancy was terminated early time and time again. We agreed it was the stress of the job, but I knew that wasn't the only reason. Of course Darius blamed me, and he was right. I was stressed, but in a situation like mine who wouldn't be?

Getting sick of hearing about how happy my friends were, and having to fake my own happiness, I got up to grab a cup of punch from off the table. Both me and my friend Michelle were on the police force; her husband was a cop also. Michelle and I went through boot camp together, and became fast friends. She met her husband on the force and I met mine in a damn club.

As a result of our occupation a lot of our coworkers were in attendance for the festivities. I had to pretend like I was happy because I didn't need them in my business asking questions. I couldn't even confide in Michelle because I was scared she would say something.

While standing at the table I got lost in thought remembering the times when we used to be happy like this. Before the first black eye he gave me, and the first lie I had to tell about how I got it. Before the first time he punched me like I was a man out in the street, and the first promise I got that it wouldn't happen again if I stayed. Before the first child was lost, and I wasn't even comforted, just beat near death because it made him look like less of a man to his friends in his eyes. Before I had to fix the problem; before I became nonexistent.

"See something you like?" Darius spoke low into my ear, sneaking up on me from behind. He had a tight grip on my already-sore waistline from the beating I endured last week, but I kept a straight face. Nobody could really know what was going on.

"What are you talking about? I'm just having a glass of punch," I whispered back, smiling as a few coworkers walked by so they wouldn't suspect my obvious discomfort.

"You've been standing here staring at dude for the past two minutes. Do you want that nigga?"

"Darius, I wasn't even looking his way. I was standing here thinking about what I would do for you for our anniversary," I quickly lied to try to take some of the heat off the subject. There was a time when I could calculate whether I would be getting dealt with later, but lately I could hardly pinpoint it. It was like I was dealing with a monster.

"That's bullshit and you know it."

"But, Darius, I was only—"

"Shut up. Know that's your ass when we get home."

He gave me a hard pinch that was sure to leave another bruise on my already-sore lower back before he walked away to engage in a loud conversation with some of the other guys at the party. My hand began to shake slightly, and I set my glass down so no one would notice. He only had about nine drinks so I was hoping he would have a few more. Maybe he would pass out and forget once we got home. I thought for sure if he gave me the chance I could fuck him to sleep, and we would be on somewhat good terms again.

Taking a seat on the couch, I pretended like I was into the conversation the women were having around me, laughing at the appropriate time, and crying on the inside because I was nearing my breaking point. *I can't deal with this anymore.*

When she tried to pass me her baby I denied it, faking like I couldn't handle holding a child, and to some point that statement was true. I couldn't handle holding her bundle of joy knowing I would probably never have the chance to hold my own. I saw Darius watching me from the other side of the room, and I didn't want to give him any more reasons to swing on me later, so I cradled the child to my chest and smiled.

Much too soon the party was over and we wished the happy couple well, accompanied by fake smiles and rushed conversation on his part as we walked down the semi-dark street to our car. Well, my car actually, but I didn't want to argue the point. My coworkers thought it was romantic that he dropped me off and came to pick me up from work every day, but that wasn't by choice. Those were the rules so that he would know I wasn't seeing anyone else.

I was quiet on the ride home, and I silently hoped the rest of the night would be the same. He sang along with the radio every so often if a song he liked came on as we made our way across town. He seemed genuinely happy as we recapped some events from the party here and there while we waited for a light to change, and I thought for four seconds that maybe God actually heard me this time and I was off the hook tonight.

When we pulled up to the garage I waited until the car was at a complete stop and I counted to ten in my head to make sure he was done parking the car before I moved to take my seat belt off. Before I could look for the key to the door he grabbed me by the bottom half of my face and whipped my head around to face him. The grip he had on my face was so tight I knew for sure if I had a glass jaw it would be broken right now. I didn't dare blink an eye or let a tear drop because he fed off of that, and tonight I couldn't handle it anymore.

"So you like looking at other niggas, huh?" he asked me through drunken eyelids, not really wanting an answer. I couldn't answer if I wanted to because of the grip he had on my jaw, and I was barely breathing as it was.

I looked him straight in the eye waiting to see what he would do next. With his free hand he unzipped his pants and pulled out his dick, stroking it into an erection while never taking his eyes from mine. *Lord, I just want it all to end . . . please.*

"If I don't cum in five minutes that's your ass," he said before forcing my mouth toward his erection. A part of me wanted to bite the bitch off and spit it in his face, but I knew I wouldn't be able to get out of the car fast enough to save my life so I obliged. Sucking his dick like he was paying me for it, and hoping that it would be enough to get me out of an ass whipping for tonight, I put in work like my life depended on it. In all actuality it did.

Up and down, around and back down again, I worked him until two and a half minutes into it I was swallowing his thick cum down my throat and making sure to lick up any excess that may have dripped from the corner of my mouth. He had a tight grip on the back of my neck, and even though I was done I had to wait until it was okay for me to move before I did so. I didn't feel like his fist caressing my face in the driveway this evening.

After an additional two and a half minutes he let me sit up, and I waited until he got himself together before I reached for my pocketbook. Feeling inside for the house keys while I waited for him to come around and open my door, my fingertips ran across the butt of my nickel-plated .22 and the pamphlet the nurse gave me at the emergency room with numbers for help when I was ready. It was no bigger than an ATM card, and fit right in the side pocket of my Dooney & Bourke bag. I just wasn't sure which I was ready to use yet: the hotline number for abused women, or a nice shiny bullet from my gun.

He finally opened my door for me, because I wouldn't dare open that shit myself and not allow him to be a man. The last time I did that the end result was my arm being slammed in the doorjamb repeatedly until it broke in two places, and us having to take a trip over to Fitzgerald Mercy hospital because we had already been to Lankenau twice that month.

I got out and hurried to open the door so that I could run upstairs before he had a chance to swing on me. I got into the house unscathed, and set my pocketbook on the kitchen counter, not really worried because my gun was hidden in a compartment beneath the material in the bottom of my overfilled bag. If I was smart I would've taken the bag upstairs with me, but I didn't think he would look in it for anything.

I ran upstairs to the room and slipped into a nightie, being sure to take my panties off because he wanted easy access at all times and didn't want to have to fight through no drawers to get what belonged to him. I lay down in the bed to wait for him to tell me I could go to sleep.

Ten minutes had passed and my eyelids were getting heavy. I figured I could close my eyes for a split second because I would be able to hear him coming down the hall. That dude must have been wearing clouds for shoes because the next time I saw him he was snatching me out the bed by my ponytail and dragging me across the room. I wanted to scream but that would just make it worse. That didn't stop the tears coming from my eyes as I asked him over and over again, "What did I do?"

Does he embarrass you in front of friends and family? Does he control your every move? Does he make all of the decisions for the household, not giving you any say? Does he hit you? Does he prevent you from going out alone?

"So you're in an abusive relationship, huh? My love ain't enough for you, Simone? What you gonna do? Leave me now?"

"Darius, please let me go. What are you talking about? I'm not going to leave you, baby," I said, trying to make sense of the situation. He definitely caught me slipping on this one because had I stayed up a second longer I would have been more prepared to duck his advances toward me.

"You're not leaving me? Then what's this, huh? What the fuck is this?" he asked, holding up the small pamphlet that I thought I hid in my pocketbook from the hospital.

I couldn't come up with a lie fast enough before he was all over me, kicking and punching me like a madman, and all I could do was ball up in the corner and try to cover my face. If only I could get to my pocketbook I could fix this. . . .

Does he hit you? Does he promise to get help? Does he embarrass you in front of family and friends? Does he go into drunken fits? Does he isolate you from your loved ones? Does he intimidate you with weapons? Does he give you a curfew? We'll keep asking until the violence stops. . . .

2

When a Man Loves a Woman

I woke up the next morning feeling like I got into a fight with Mike Tyson. My head was pounding, and there was a constant ringing in my left ear that I couldn't shake. I wanted to open both eyes, but my right one was swollen shut. Chancing a glance with my one functioning eye, I glanced around the room to determine my next move. From my prone position the scan of my surroundings first landed on the patch of hair that he ripped from my scalp mere hours before. There was blood splattered on the wall from, I was sure, my busted lip and nose, which I wasn't quite sure was broken. The pamphlet that caused all of the drama lay on the floor in a million tiny pieces along with my ripped nightgown and one slipper. *Lord only knows where the mate may be.*

I closed my one good eye and listened to my surroundings. I didn't hear any heavy breathing next to me, so that meant that Darius had already gotten up and started his day. By now, I was sure, he had already called the precinct to inform them that I wasn't feeling too good, and would be taking the next few days off. There was a bubble bath ready where he would try to wash the bruises away; and a semi-hot breakfast would be waiting for me in the kitchen on the table decorated with fresh tiger lilies and the morning paper. A cushion would be in my chair because it would be too painful for my sore rear to make direct contact with the cherry wood of my kitchen furniture.

Today we would go shopping after he carefully positioned my sore body into a sweat suit because anything else would press against me and be uncomfortable. He would stand off to the side as I applied makeup, afterward carefully inspecting my face to make sure I'd covered any telltale signs of a fight. He couldn't have people staring at my bruised face and knowing our business, after all. He would remind me to grab my sunglasses, and we would be off for the day pretending like we were happy, perpetrating a fraud for the world to see.

This was routine, and to be expected. Darius never changed, and it was almost like I knew what would happen next before he did. Why I never used this intuition to my advantage I'd never know. It was a tiring routine nonetheless, and unhealthy on top of all that. Maybe today I could actually talk him into getting some help, but I would just have to see how the day went. Darius was pretty predictable, but he was just as unpredictable and his mood could swing to the left at a moment's notice. I'd see how the day went, but know that my hopes weren't set high for a positive outcome. I could never get too hype about shit with Darius because you just never really knew how things would turn out with him.

I could only hope that God finally granted my prayers, and my day would be totally different. Today would be the day I got out of the bed and I would see the hair in the corner, the blood on the wall, and my tattered belongings. I would swing my sore body around to the side of the bed, and drag my naked body to the bathroom. Upon looking in the mirror I would be instantly reminded of how Tina Turner looked in *What's Love Got to Do with It,* but my face would be worse off than hers was after the limo scene. I would shrug my sore body into my bathrobe and make my way down to the kitchen, where the smell of freshly brewed coffee got stronger as I approached.

I would walk into the kitchen and see Darius's body slumped over at the kitchen table, with a pool of dark blood dripping from the table and collecting on the floor from the self-inflicted gunshot wound to the head with my .22 in his cold, dead fingers. I would sit down after pouring my cup of coffee and feel relief as I drank my hot beverage, enjoying it probably much longer than I should, and then I'd dial 911 on my cell phone. I would sound cool and calm as I told the operator that a dead man was at my table, and they should come get him. I would *not* wipe the smile off my face when they showed up to claim his lifeless body. *I'll be free.*

Unfortunately the heavy sound of boots, more than likely the ones used to stomp me into the floor, could be heard from the hall, and I tried to act like I was still sleeping. As loud as his steps were, it was bizarre how I didn't hear him coming last night. One of two things could go down this morning. He could still be in a bad mood from last night and the fight would continue, or he would be in a good mood for some odd reason and the day would go as previously described. More often than not the next day was way better than the day before. He wasn't overly excited the next day, but he did tend to be very apologetic and willing to do whatever it was that would make me happy. Just know that I was in no rush to find out either way. I didn't feel like having to fake being happy with him when my body would no doubt be still sore and I had a pounding headache on my hands. I fought to keep my body from tensing up as he approached the bed, and I could feel his presence looming over me like a dark cloud on a sunny day. *I fucking hate him.*

"Simone, wake up, baby. It's already after ten. . . ." he said in a calm voice as he bent first at the knees then the

waist to get down to eye level. It was after ten, so he had
definitely already made the call to the gig. I was supposed
to be there by eight. I opened up one eye, and struggled to
open the other, but it hurt too badly. A tear escaped, and
I flinched a little as he raised his hand to wipe it away.
Never show weakness, and tears were a definite sign. His
touch was soft, unlike the Incredible Hulk–like fists that
crashed down into my face hours ago, and I calmed down
for a brief second.

I struggled to sit up, and I allowed him to assist me
because I really couldn't do it myself. Searing sparks of
pain shot through my back, and a slight thump played a
peculiar beat at my right temple. My feet felt like I had
cement cinderblocks attached at the ankles, and the rest
of my body sagged like an old bag of bones. I was feeling
defeated, and afraid to face the day. He gently picked me
up from the bed and carried me into my custom-made
bathroom, where he softly placed me on the toilet so that
I could relieve myself. He kind of gave me privacy by
turning his back, but he didn't leave the room.

As soon as the sound from the stream of urine stopped,
he turned back around, not even giving me a chance to
wipe. He flushed the toilet, and tenderly lifted me again
and submerged my body in rose-scented water. He knew
these bath salts almost always gave me a yeast infection,
but I didn't have the energy to even bring it up again. That
would just be another argument where he thought I was
trying to control him, or he thought I thought he didn't
know how to take care of me. I slid down until the water
covered my shoulders, resisting the urge to go all the way
down and stay there until my last breath was snatched
from my lungs. I closed my eyes and let the nearly too-hot
water relax my body.

He wetted a thick washcloth with the rose-scented
water, wrung it out tightly, and placed it over my face.

The scent relaxed me. He did this a few more times until I could finally open my sealed right eye. It burned like hell when the light hit it, but I fought through the pain so that he could see his progress. I'd realized that in the healing process after a fight, it made it easier on me if he could sense that I knew he was trying to make up for what he did. He had yet to start swinging on me again if things didn't go in his favor, but his attitude was the worse if he felt like I was not grateful for his actions. This was a part of the ritual, and if done correctly I'd make it through the day hopefully without incident. It was still early, so right now I was just trying to stay on top of my game.

He soaped the rag and took his time removing dried and clotted blood from the sides of my mouth and under my nose, afterward checking for loose teeth. Thankfully they were all still holding strong. He then took the rag across my nose, and although it was very painful, it didn't feel broken. I was thankful because that meant I wouldn't have to sit in the emergency room and make up more lies. He took his time rinsing and soaping as his journey went farther down my body, and he let the water out slowly as he traveled until he got to my feet, and I was just a soapy form lying before him. Removing the detachable showerhead, he adjusted the water until the temperature was right, and proceeded to rinse me until all of the soap was gone. Grabbing the fluffiest towel we owned, he gathered my naked form out of the tub, and took me to the room. I felt my muscles starting to relax some, and I was able to move around slowly on my own.

To be honest with you, I was in my head heavy during this entire process. I wondered how many times I would have to go through this process before he actually succeeded in killing me. The truth was, I didn't think he actually wanted me to die. He just didn't really know how to show me love in any other form. I wanted to believe that he loved me simply because every time I wanted to call it quits he begged so hard for me to stay. He'd been able to convince me several times that he would change if I stayed and helped him. I always felt like we were making progress, and just when I thought we had gotten over the hump, we were right back at scratch. *This shit is getting old . . . fast.*

Once in the room he set me gently on the bed, and I avoided the mirrors for as long as I could because eventually I was going to have to get a good look at myself. He watched me closely, but stayed quiet as I limped around the room at a snail's pace to gather my personal belongings on the bed. He already had Juicy Couture sweats out, along with a pair of Ugg boots. I did my best to dry off, making sure I got as much of the water off as I could without hurting myself, because I didn't want him to think I was purposely trying to catch a cold by not drying off properly. We'd been through this enough times for me to know the routine, and I didn't need for him to go accusing me for some imaginary shit in his head. What I really wanted to do was sleep for a few more hours, but I knew he wasn't even having that. The last time I tried to go back to sleep after a bath and we were supposed to be going out, we ended up in another fight that left me bruised even worse than the night before. Do know that I learned from the experience.

By the time I was ready to step into my clothes the now-gentle giant crossed the room in three enormous steps and assisted me. I let him do his thing, carefully applying my MAC face afterward. I was taken back a little by my face. This was the worst beating by far, and I had to slow down and take my time to make sure everything was concealed well. I was crying so hard on the inside, but I knew better than to let a tear drop. Once my face was set and I had his approval, we took the party to the kitchen soon after.

Just like I thought, breakfast was on a hot plate ready for me to dig in. My pocketbook was on the counter where I left it, with a few of my belongings scattered across the top. He held the chair as I stiffly bent to take a seat, and once I was settled he sat in the seat to my left and sipped a cup of black coffee as he chuckled at the comics. I could only wish that I had ground some glass up and stirred it in his cup like sugar, but today wasn't my lucky day. I ate breakfast quick, and upon finishing I placed my fork back on my plate, and folded my hands into my lap, staying quiet until he was done.

He got up, grabbed our jackets, helped me in mine, and we were ready to get the day rolling. Although I favored my left foot, I tried to make my limp appear as minimal as possible so as not to draw attention. While he got the keys to my truck I waited by the door.

"Simone . . . you know I love you right?" he spoke to me in a calm voice.

"Yes, I know. . . ."

"And you know I will never hurt you on purpose. I was drunk last night," he spoke, guilt blanketing his face like a sheen of sweat.

"Yes, I know. . . ."

"Just don't leave me, okay? Today I'll make it up to you."

I didn't bother to respond. I mean, respond for what? We'd already been here so many times, and he had already failed to stick to the promise of getting better. Shopping sprees were not making up for the bumps and bruises and the lies I had to live on a daily basis to keep my secret. I wanted my husband back. The one I met years ago who was so attentive and so affectionate. Not this monster I was stuck with now. I wanted to leave him, I really did, but a part of me felt like I could help him and we could get back to how things used to be. I thought a baby would help, but he kept beating them out of me. There was a solution, I was sure of it. I just had to figure it all out.

I waited for him to open the door, and I stepped outside and to the right to give him room to lock it. I wouldn't dare take a step down the driveway without him. The last time I did that he thought the guy next door was looking at me too long, and I got beat for nothing that night, too. Staying in my lane, I waited for my husband, my king, my protector to escort me to my chariot and drive me off into the sunset . . . or over a high cliff. Whichever would take me from this misery the fastest. There had to be a way out, and I could only hope I found it before it was too late.

3

What's Love Without Tragedy

I used to love him a long time ago when things were more light and carefree. By now you're probably wondering why I hadn't killed this fool yet. After all, I was an officer of the law and could surely justify his death with the beatings, right? I mean, why didn't I just leave his trifling ass and take my life back? I'd been asking myself those very same questions for the past year.

Something in me felt like he needed me. He had told me in the past how he was hurt by women he loved unconditionally, and for one reason or another they never returned the love to him the way he gave it. He had serious trust issues, and it was a struggle for us for a while when we first hooked up. I felt like I had to prove to him that I wasn't like those other women who hurt him, and that I would never leave him hanging. I promised him that we would always work through our issues, and that it was truly for better or worse. Who knew that the worst part of it would last so long?

Not that this made the situation any better, but for the sake of argument Darius wasn't always like this. When we first met it was lust at first sight. He was a double shot of mocha energy wrapped in Armani, and from my view on the other side of the club I knew I would be taking him home with me at the end of the night. Me and a few sistas from the force were out celebrating our completion of boot camp, getting hired at the same precinct, and finally earning our badges. There were only four females on the male-dominant lineup, and they took us through hell and high water but we made it through at the top of the class. Surely a reason to get our party on and ball out a little, right?

One of the other women I was out with had her eye on him, but I wasn't even worried about the competition. He was giving me the same energy I was putting out, and I knew it was only a matter of time before we connected. The deal was sealed when she called herself, making her presence known, but he didn't even give her a second glance. His eyes stayed locked on my body the entire time. I was a lady so I wasn't about to just throw myself at him, but when my favorite song came on I got up to hit the dance floor, and he followed suit, meeting me in the middle.

It was just like on TV, and the room went black with tunnel vision and we could only see each other. He seemingly floated toward me, and as I dropped it low and swept the floor with it, like my girl Beyoncé said, we were in sync and loving it. When I dipped right he dipped right too, and when I backed it up he was right there catching all I had to offer him through my tight skirt with my wide hips. In between dances we tossed back a few shots, but as soon as the deejay put on a song we liked we were right back on the dance floor, setting the place on fire. I soon forgot that I even came there with my girls as I danced the night away with Prince Charming.

By the end of the night I was a little tipsy, but aware. I didn't hesitate when he offered to follow me home to make sure I arrived safely. I wasn't worried because everyone saw us together, and I let my girl Michelle know that we were leaving together . . . just in case. When we pulled up to my house he was the perfect gentleman. I must say it was a little disappointing. I was hoping to be penned against the door as I wrestled to get my key in the lock. Once we finally got inside he would press me against the other side, and we would wildly kiss our way out of our clothes. Those clothes would have led up to the bedroom where we would stop briefly to add protection, and then I would ride him into the night and well into the next morning where I would wake up to the smell of breakfast in bed like Larenz Tate did for Nia Long in the movie *Love Jones*. That would have only led to a round four where I would blow his mind in more ways than he could imagine and then we would part ways.

The shit didn't even happen like that, and he turned out to be a complete gentleman. I had to give him cool points for that though. At least he offered me the chance to continue being a lady, and who knew that it would turn into a great courtship? When we got to the door he gave me a kiss on the cheek and a quick hug before plugging his number into my phone. He didn't pull off until I was locked securely in the house and was upstairs in my bedroom. I guessed chivalry wasn't dead after all.

I was a little irked because I was left hot and ready to fuck, but the one I wanted to give it to didn't even want it. It was cool, though. Since he wanted to make me sweat . . . well let the games begin. I was tired as hell and a little hung over the next day, but I managed to make it to the precinct on time the next morning. As soon as I walked in the door Michelle flashed the widest smile my way. I loved Michelle, and even though we put our lives on the line on a consistent basis, she was the best partner in the world and made it all worthwhile.

"Giiiirrrrlllll . . . tell me you crawled all over that man last night," she said as we embraced. Unlike a few of my other colleagues, Michelle and I were on the same page and didn't waste time wasting time. Our motto: if you like it go for it. If it works, then good for you. If it doesn't, then on to the next one. Those were our rules to live by. It saved us a lot of heartache in the long run.

"Honey, no. He was a true gentleman and dropped my horny ass right at the door," I said with a little agitation in my voice.

"They still exist?" she said to me with a straight face. As soon as she said it we busted out laughing. Michelle always had a way of lightening the mood.

"Chile, apparently there are a few of them still left out there. Just my damn luck, one found me. I was ready to suck the skin off that thing last night!"

We were cracking up as we made our way into the boardroom for our morning meeting. Normally two women weren't paired up, just in case things got way out of control, but Michelle and I graduated numbers one and two, respectively, out of our class, and were hired at the same precinct, where we petitioned to be partners as soon as we were allowed. Initially we had to partner up with a veteran officer to learn the ropes, but once our captain felt we were prepared to be together he allowed it. It'd been working for us ever since.

We sat and whispered in the corner up until Andre walked in. I wasn't really paying much attention until I realized I was having a one-sided conversation with Michelle because she wasn't answering.

"Girl, did you . . . Ohhhh, Andre in the building!"

"Girl, hush." She giggled as she blushed and tried not to look his way. We were all in training together, and she'd always had a thing for him. He was obviously pretty smitten with her as well, so I wasn't sure what the holdup was. Maybe he was another one of those rare chivalrous-type dudes we thought we didn't want. Andre was a sweetheart though, and very shy. You couldn't tell that by the way he handled criminals on the regular, but he definitely had a soft spot for Michelle, and everyone could see it.

As the briefing started, hating-ass Sharla from last night came sliding in, and took a seat next to me. I could still see the salt on her face from when she saw homeboy leaving with me, but just like the previous evening I still wasn't paying her ass any mind. Hell, he wasn't my man. If she could get his ass she could have him. It was obvious to both of us who he wanted, but she still could give it a go.

"Hey, girl, I saw you leave with ol' boy last night," she leaned over and whispered in my ear as the captain was going over detail.

"Mmmm hmmm," I dryly responded as I attempted to give my captain my full attention. Shit, we just got hired there, and I didn't want to make any mistakes my first day on the job. Being hired right out of the academy was a blessing, and I wanted my captain toknow I wanted to be there.

"Chile, I looked into him when I left the club last night. I wouldn't fool with him if I was you."

The look on my face said everything. Was this chick that thirsty and alone that she didn't have anything else to do but run records on strangers? Wow, the dating game must have changed since the last time I was on the scene because I didn't think I was that serious.

"Oh yeah? Why would you say that?"

"He's an abuser. Has a history of beating his women. He has a few charges from about five years ago."

"Oh okay, thanks for the info."

I kept quiet the rest of the meeting, but Sharla definitely had me thinking. I had a gun that I wasn't afraid to use, but the guy I met last night couldn't be the same guy Sharla was just talking about. Mr. Nice Guy? I had a hard time processing it, and told Michelle that when we got into our squad car to roll out for the day, practically dragging Michelle out afterward so we could talk.

"You know from experience that abusers don't always come with a stamp on their head. Did she have papers on him?" Michelle asked as we pulled into the Dunkin' Donuts drive-through.

"No, she didn't, but knowing Sharla she ain't have nothing else to do but look his ass up."

"I'll just say this. If you like him, do you. He may have had a shady past, but could be a changed person. You said yourself that last charge was five years ago. Abusers don't normally take a hiatus. That situation could be totally misconstrued. Hell, all you want is a good fuck anyway. Get it and get ghost!"

We fell out laughing, and I felt totally at ease. *I know the signs of abuse, and I know how to protect myself so I'm not worried.* Hell, we've all done some shady shit in the past that seemed worse off than it really was. I decided to see what Mr. Nice Guy was about before writing him off completely. *Who knows? He may just turn out to be right what I need.*

4

Consider Yourself Warned

Statistics show that one out of four women is abused on a daily basis, and roughly 4,000 die each year from it. 30 percent of women report to know someone who has been a victim of abuse, but only about 9 percent actually report it before it's too late. The thing about abuse is not every abused woman is walking around looking battered. Abuse comes in many forms. Just your mate calling you a bitch on the regular is abuse if it's not a form of foreplay. I never thought I would be in that category, but that's exactly where I found myself a few years after Darius and I started dating.

I decided to go ahead and see what Darius was about. He was a gentleman by all means. He looked good . . . smelled good . . . and we had a ball together. At first I was on a straight mission to get bedded, but this dude really wanted to court me. Something that didn't go down like that in this day and age. Shit, leave it to Facebook: if you like my picture you're my boyfriend. So this actually wanting to date and get to know me was new and exciting, and I liked it.

I quickly forgot about the warning Sharla gave and dove right into Darius's world and let him treat me the way I deserved to be treated in his eyes. He had me convinced that I was a queen and deserved the finer things in life, and I believed him since my daddy had been telling me just that since I was a little girl. I got flowers once a week and like clockwork we met up for brunch every Saturday that I wasn't working. He even started picking me up in the morning and taking me to work, only to return after work to make sure I got home on a daily basis because I was "precious cargo." This man made me feel special, and I was so giddy over him. Michelle was feeling the same sparks with Andre so we were geeked out most of the time with dreamy looks on our faces while we waited for some dumb ass to commit a crime.

Finally, I had found someone who was the ultimate package, and it felt good. We had been kicking it for a few months by this point, and everything was on the rise. The only thing was we hadn't slept together yet, and I was confused a little by it. I was ready to drop the pussy on him, but he kept pushing me off, saying that the time would present itself when it was supposed to happen. *I wanted it to happen five months, six days, three hours, nine minutes, and forty-two seconds ago, but who is counting?*

"What if he has a small dick, and that's why he's holding off? All of this time would be wasted," I grumbled and complained to Michelle as we worked out at the station. We had to stay tight and right to be able to chase these fools down in the street, and we always kept to our workout schedule. I hated a fat cop, and refused to fall into the lazy cop crew.

"Chile, when you love someone it's not the size of the boat that makes the difference. Shit, the Titanic wasn't even reliable, and at the end of the day they had to depend on a tugboat to save their asses."

Michelle . . . you gotta love her. Maybe that's why things in her life were so easygoing. In this field of work you had to live carefree because all we had was our faith on these streets. Home shit could be a distraction that could cost you your life. A lesson none of us wanted to learn.

"Well, how long are you and Andre going to wait? Things with y'all have been getting a little heavy I noticed," I replied, slightly out of breath as I slowed to a smooth jog on the treadmill. It felt like forever had passed before she answered, and when I looked over she was trying to avoid eye contact.

"You fast ho!" I yelled at her through my smile. "So, you got the dick and you didn't tell me? How could you?"

"Girl, it was everything, you hear me? It just kind of happened one day . . . and been happening ever since. I think he's the one, Simone. I really do."

All I could do was smile for my friend as I stopped my treadmill and moved to give her a hug. We had been talking about finding true love since the day we met, and finally we had both found someone we wanted to be with for better or worse. We chatted nonstop, stopping to shower, and then kept the conversation going on our cell phones as our men drove us home. Darius insisted in chauffeuring me on a daily, and Michelle and Andre took turns carpooling. We were ecstatic things were going the way we planned. We had to be the luckiest women on the face of the earth.

Michelle and I ended our conversation just short of reaching our destinations, and as I prepared to lean over and give Darius a kiss good night he was preparing to get out as well. Normally he would lean in, kiss me, and wait until I was in the house safely unless it was our date night or he was helping me with groceries. I was a little taken aback by the change of plans, but I didn't say a word. I just went with the flow and sat back to see how it would go down.

He came around the other side of the car, wrapping me in a loving embrace followed up by the most sensual

kiss I'd ever experienced. I was breathless by the time
he pulled his lips from mine, but I didn't say a word. I
wasn't sure I would be able to control my attitude if a
dicking didn't go down tonight, so I kept my hormones in
check the best I could. He wasn't normally this up close
and personal, but I wasn't about to complain. I had been
hinting at just this thing for months.

When we got inside he excused himself and went to
the bathroom. I set my tired body down on the couch,
waiting for him to come back. Tonight wasn't the night he
normally came over so I wasn't necessarily prepared for
anything, and was planning to eat salad for dinner. When
he came back down he motioned for me to follow him
upstairs. Playing along, I removed my tired form from the
couch and followed him. We ended up in the bathroom,
where he had run a bath for me complete with petals on
top of the water and all. A fluffy towel sat on the side of
the sink, and a bottle of champagne was on ice in the sink.
I didn't even remember him bringing in bags so when did
he have time to do all of this?

"I know you gave me the key for emergency purposes,
but I wanted to do something nice for you to show my
appreciation for having you in my life. Tonight, I'm going
to take care of you."

Speechless once again . . . and take care of me he did. It
started with him taking off my clothes slowly, kissing my
skin as it became exposed. By the time he got down on his
knees to remove my panties I couldn't help but throw a
leg over his shoulder and hope he didn't brush me off this
time. When I felt the tip of his tongue swirl around my
overly sensitive clit I knew for sure it was going to be on
and popping tonight.

He stopped just short of me coating his tongue with
my creamy goodness, and my body was still shaking as
he lifted me and placed me in the tub. The water was

damn near scalding, just the way I liked it, and it felt like a warm body wrapped entirely around me. He stepped out of the bathroom for a quick second, and came back naked from the waist up. I couldn't wait to see what he was working with.

He stooped beside the tub and soaped the rag up, rubbing and teasing my body with it as he cleansed my skin. He would let the water out a little at a time until all of the water was gone, and I was completely covered in bubbles. Standing to grab the showerhead, he used his bare hands to aid in rinsing the soap from me, lingering longer in other places than most until I was rinsed clean. Afterward he scooped my naked body up and carried me into the room, where he placed me gently on the side of the bed.

Stepping back he watched as I applied a scented cream to my body, and didn't come back to the bed until I was done. Leaning down in front of me on the side of the bed he parted my legs with his strong hands, inhaling me as he leaned in. Gently, he placed my legs across his shoulders and as soon as my back made contact with the blanket his tongue touched me and had me singing in falsetto.

It was like we were moving in slow motion. In the midst of all of that was happening he somehow became naked. I was so busy trying to get away from his mouth that before I knew it I had scooted up to the top of the bed, and was holding on the headboard for dear life. He had both hands holding my legs back by the back of my thighs, and his tongue was steadily diving in and out of me, scooping my cream up in the process. His hands felt hot, like they were searing my skin and leaving a burning trail behind. It was sauna hot in the room, and I didn't think I could fly any higher. I wanted to feel this man all over me but I couldn't speak the words. He must have been telepathic because he moved right where I needed him to be.

He slowly crawled up my body, kissing me on every

reachable spot along the way. My body jerked involuntarily, and my eyes strained to see the package. This man was really holding out on letting me see the goods, and I wanted to at least get a taste before it all went down.

"Darius, slow down . . . let me taste you. Let me return the favor," I moaned out as he covered my body with his. He hesitated for a split second, but thankfully he scooped me up and rolled until my body was on top of his and I sat straddling him.

It was like my clit had a heartbeat and I could feel the pulse against his thickness. I prayed that it wasn't just thick and had some length to it. I wanted to rush down there to see what I was working with, but I returned the same courtesy and took my time kissing his entire body, pausing a moment to swirl my tongue around his nipples before trailing kisses down the center of his torso. I was salivating and couldn't wait to get to the prize.

I stopped at his thick pubic region and inhaled deeply, taking in his scent. He smelled freshly bathed and delicious. When I finally leaned up to reveal the package, I couldn't have been happier. Not only was it thick, this man was hanging. A nice long piece of chocolate for my tasting pleasure. I took my time suckling the head and dragging my mouth up and down the underside of his length. I deep throated him the best I could, and jerked him slow at the same time, making him even harder than before.

"Please . . . let me feel you. I can't take it anymore," Darius begged from the top of the bed. I didn't want to wait a minute longer so I skillfully rolled a condom on and climbed on top of him. Mounting him, I slid down on him an inch at a time, easing my way to the promised land. He filled me up completely, and I promise you I couldn't breathe the entire time.

He leaned up and wrapped his arms around me, rocking

me in a lazy rhythm as I worked his pole in and out of me, being sure to tap my G-spot every time. He was grinding into me, putting pressure on my clit every time we got close, and I wasn't sure if I was going to be able to hold out much longer.

"You ready to be mine forever?" he spoke low into my ear as we began to reach a climax.

"Yes . . ."

"Say you'll never leave me," he demanded as he stroked me deeper, pulling my body in closer to his.

"I won't leave . . ."

"I won't let you."

The feeling that flowed through my body felt like I was surely taking my last breath. I couldn't believe what was happening as my body convulsed and a stream of honey coated us both as I screamed out. I had been waiting forever for this moment, and if good things surely came to those who waited then great things would come to those who waited the longest. Darius had officially turned my world upside down, and it was only a matter of time before I found out how deep it would truly get.

5

That's the Way Love Goes

"Do you forgive me? I mean, for what I did last night? Did today make it better?" Darius questioned me as we sat in the food court at the King of Prussia Mall. For someone who seemed to exude so much power he was very weak and insecure, and always needed validation. One of those things that you don't find out until way later into the relationship.

The chair was so uncomfortable that it was hard to concentrate on my food, but I knew better than to show discomfort in public so I thugged it out the best I could while I picked at my Saladworks salad. Rarely was I allowed to eat processed foods, and today wasn't one of those days. Normally after we got into a fight he would allow me to get whatever I wanted to eat, but today when I moved to stand in the Chick-fil-A line he leaned in and whispered in my ear that it looked like I was picking up weight. I wanted to put up a fight because I really wanted a brownie, but I didn't feel like getting beat once we got home so I reluctantly followed him to Saladworks, where he put together a salad for me full of shit I didn't like. I forced myself to eat some of it so that he wouldn't feel like he was wasting his money, but I really didn't want it and really didn't feel like going through the motions.

"Yeah, I forgive you. . . ." I straight lied to him, making eye contact and flashing a slight smile, hoping that he believed me. Hell no, I didn't forgive his ass, and I wished in my head that at the very moment a pack of wild orangutans would come through the mall and mangle his tired ass. I just wanted him to die, and knew one day it would have to be decided if it was going to be me or him. I never would have thought in my wildest dreams that I would feel like I did toward him, but it just goes to show that no matter how long you know somebody you never really know them and they always have a surprise up their sleeve.

"You just make me so mad sometimes, and I know what I did to you was wrong. I'm going to look into that therapy session you were telling me about, too. Watch, I'm going to be a changed person." He talked nonstop, looking like he really wanted me to believe him this time. I wanted to tell his simple ass I didn't believe him, but I decided to let him be great as I continued to pick at my food. I suggested therapy to Darius maybe the third beating in, when I felt like he was really trying to kill me. He cried and begged me to stay as I packed a bag to go stay at Michelle's until he got his shit together. This was when the beatings started to get really bad, but I felt like I still had some sort of control. He said he would do anything for me to stay. I was still waiting for a therapy session to happen.

"I know you are. Are you ready to go?" I asked as I pushed my food to the center of the table, and pulled my cell phone out to check my face in the mirrored reflection. It looked like some of the swelling had gone down some, but it still looked a little puffy around my nose. I just wanted to go take a nap and hopefully with a warm compress I could get the swelling down within the next few days.

He didn't look too happy about me rushing him, but at this point he can't hurt me no more than he already had. I

didn't have any more fight left in me, all the love I had for
him was gone, and true story I just wanted to go lie down
for a while and get my life. I was exhausted and needed
some sleep. I was stooped down trying to gather my bags
from my feet when I heard a male voice approaching
call out my name. I sat up instantly, hoping that he had
the wrong person because I didn't feel like another of
Darius's jealous fits.

"Simone, that is you. How have you been? I haven't
seen you in forever."

I looked up to stare into the eyes of an old flame from
too many years ago to count. He still looked good, too.
We broke up because I was going into the police force and
he was leaving to become a navy man. I didn't want to go
with him. I probably should have because he was good to
me, and nothing like the bullshit I had with Darius.

"Hi, Chris, how have you been? It's good to see you," I
replied in shock. I was even more in shock when he leaned
over and scooped me up in a tight embrace that hurt like
hell. I pushed back off of him instantly, but the look on
Darius's face said everything. If I didn't clear this shit up
soon that would be my ass once we got in the parking lot.

"You look gorgeous," Chris went on as he smiled at
me like he wanted to eat me up right there. It felt like
everything went into slow motion for a second and I
couldn't breathe.

"Chris, this is my husband, Darius. Darius, this is—"

"Hello, Chris, it's nice to meet you." Darius got up,
giving Chris a firm handshake that caused him to wince
in pain a little. Darius was flexing his muscles and trying
to prove a point, and I could only hope this little situation
didn't get out of hand.

"Likewise," Chris replied, shaking his hand a little.
"Well, Simone, I'm not going to keep you. Maybe I'll see
you around?" he replied as he flashed me another bright

smile. He had me melting on the inside, and I hoped it didn't show on my face.

"Ummm . . . yeah, sure. Enjoy the rest of your day."

Without looking at Darius I gathered the numerous bags from Intimacy, Arden B, 7 For All Mankind, Ann Taylor, Bijou Avenue, Bare Minerals, and Blooming-dale's. He had to know that this wasn't my fault and there was no way I would run into someone I knew on purpose. After all, the glasses were supposed to cover my face and make me unrecognizable, but he didn't get that I still looked like me and didn't have a completely different face even with makeup.

By the time we quickly walked through the mall and got to the car I could see that he was livid, but I didn't do anything this time around. When I finally caught up with him he held the trunk door up so that I could put my bags inside of it and moved to open my door. I quickly scooted into my seat, making sure that I was securely fastened as he shut my door and made his way around to the other side. I rummaged through my pocketbook, looking for a stick of gum to moisten my dry mouth, when suddenly my head crashed into the glass of the door.

"You take me there every time. What the fuck was that?" he questioned me in a rage-filled voice that scared the hell out of me. Again I fought the urge to grab my gun from my purse and splatter his brains against the other door. Why in hell would he even believe that I knew I would run into my ex? As I pondered this I had to remember that this was my insecure-ass husband I was dealing with, and I had to find a way to smooth over this situation. I really shouldn't have been this deep, but Darius magnified every damn thing, and this was no exception.

"Darius, how could you think that I knew—"

"Shut the fuck up!" He debased me as he started the car. "I saw how you looked at him. You want that nigga? Do you?"

"Darius, I barely made eye contact. He's just—"

"Somebody you used to give my pussy to. I know who the fuck he is."

"But, Darius, it wasn't—"

"I said shut the fuck up! Bitch, you must have not heard me the first time."

I clutched my bag to my chest and kept quiet. This fool was tripping off nothing, and when he got like this it was best to just ride out the storm until it was over. The funny thing was, for Darius not to want anyone else to want me he sure didn't act like he was interested in keeping me happy enough to stay with him. This was the kind of shit that happened too often to keep track, and I swear I was fed up with this shit. I had to get out and get help. There was no way this was going to pan out to be a good situation.

"You must got the game fucked up." Darius drove like a madman through the city, blurting out angry little half sentences like the situation was still mulling around in his head. I couldn't believe this shit was even happening, and it took everything in me not to reach up and press my hand against my throbbing right eye. I kept seeing little flashes of light on that side, but I just kept blinking until they went away. I didn't want any sudden movements to trigger him.

He pulled up into the driveway at full speed, barely stopping in enough time not to drive into the garage door. I was still on mute because I didn't know what this fool was going to do. He sat back in his seat and closed his eyes, periodically banging his fist into the steering wheel and streaming obscenities at no one in particular. Every so often he would give me the look of death like he wanted to squeeze the life from my body, but he didn't react and I knew enough to be quiet. This went on for at least fifteen minutes, and after a while I really had to pee. I wanted to say something to him, but I waited to see where he was going with all of this. Most times if I just stayed quiet and waited it out he would get himself together and we could at least get in the house without me being knocked out in the driveway. I didn't want to interrupt his moment and risk getting punched in the face again.

"Simone," Darius said to me in a calm voice that left me leery of his next move. "I want you to go in the house and take a nap. I'll be back in a little while."

I didn't say a word. Instead, I quickly removed my seat belt and pulled my key from the bag. I didn't even bother to try to get the bags from the back because that was not in his directions, and I didn't want to not follow his orders.

When I got inside I quickly made a trip to the bathroom, where, once I was relieved, I popped two pain pills so that I could try to get some rest. I didn't know how long he was going to be gone for, or where he was even going, but I knew if I was going to get any peace I had to be on top of my game. I stripped down to nothing and put on a sheer nightgown just in case he wanted to have sex when he came in. Once my body made contact with the bed I was asleep before I even hit the pillow.

When I woke up it was actually dark outside, and the clock showed that I had been asleep for about four hours. I wanted to go downstairs to see if Darius had come in because it was odd that he didn't even come up to the room when he got back. If nothing else, he would have at least come in the room to make sure I did what he told me to do. I had to use the restroom anyway, so I took a chance and peeped out the window only to find that my truck wasn't parked out front. I wanted to check and see if he had pulled it into the garage, but if he found me anywhere in the house other than where he told me to be that could potentially lead to another ass whipping that I could avoid by just following directions.

I started to call him but then he would think that I was trying to track his movements, so all I could do was wait. Taking my spot back in my bed, I thought about the direction my life had taken with him and how I really didn't deserve to be in this situation. Michelle and I had plans, and while her life was playing out like the fairy tale we imagined it would be, my shit was just as raggedy as it got. This was supposed to be happily ever after, but it was more like I was trapped in a horror movie as the starring actress.

I have a gun. I want to use it. Maybe today will be the day. Grabbing my bag from the side of the bed, I put my hand inside and fished around until I felt the butt of the gun on my fingertips. Why couldn't I just pull the trigger? The more I thought about it the more I wanted to just get it done and over with. Just as I thought about sliding the gun under my pillow I heard the truck pull up. Quickly zipping my pocketbook, I hung it in my closet and hopped back under the covers. He would be up here at any second, and tonight I just wanted to live. I didn't know how many more chances he had before his time was up, but it was coming. Today I decided that it would be him who lost the battle, but I was going to give him one last chance to redeem himself. Maybe I could convince him to really get help this time. It was going to be his choice because if he didn't he wasn't going to like the outcome. I was tired of being tired, and at this point I had nothing to lose.

6

Back Down Memory Lane

There are two times as many cases of reported domestic violence as reported rapes, but only about one out of ten are actually reported. Violence occurs at least once in the course of the marriage in over half of all marriages. If you cut the half in half, of these marriages, violence occurs regularly. One out of six couples in the US experiences domestic violence every year. There are at least 40,000 abused women in Philadelphia alone. Studies of violent families show that the violence escalates over time, becoming more intense and more frequent. In 8.5 percent of murders of spouses, the police have been called five or more times. The abuse is becoming more serious, and these wives are reaching out for help. Almost half of all women treated in hospital emergency rooms have injuries probably from being battered by their husband or boyfriend; at least 17 percent are definitely battered.

The crazy thing is, what do you do when you are the police? Many will say that an abused police officer is unbelievable. After all, I was the law and I had a gun so I couldn't possibly get in trouble for defending myself. "If it were me I would blast him from the door," many have said . . . even me. A lot of times the woman in the abusive relationship is too far in to back out. Either he has isolated her from her family, or has taken financial control of everything, leaving her totally dependent on him. In my case, although I brought in the bulk of the money, he had all of my bank and credit cards, and I was only allowed to use them when we were together.

He did construction, but lately he was at home more than at work because of the length of his job duties. Once they were done with a project he would sometimes be home for months before another project became available. He was in the union, and that guaranteed unemployment, but when you are making damn near forty dollars an hour, and the money that you are used to making is cut below half, that could mess with a man's ego. I should have wrapped it up the first time he went off on me, but I thought I loved him. No, I knew I loved him and I was willing to work through the tough times with him. After all, I didn't want to up and leave him when times got rough like the other women in his past did. I was willing to stay and prove that we could make it through thick and thin.

Over time I began to realize that I couldn't love him enough for both of us. I had to take control somehow and get my life back in order. I figured if I just did my very best to do what he asked me to do then everything would be okay, and somehow we would get back to how we used to be. I learned in the academy how to spot dead-on a person in an abusive relationship. We learned to recognize the telltale signs, and how to coerce the victim out and away from the target. I used what I knew to hide my own abuse from my coworkers, but it was harder to keep up the charade.

The next morning when I woke up to Darius's heavy footsteps I did as I had been taught and lay still in the bed until I could feel him standing over me. I opened up my eyes and braced myself for impact, which surprisingly never came. I was certain he would plant his huge fist in the center of my chest with enough force to knock a small child clear across the room, but instead he kneeled down beside me and looked me in the eye.

"I'm sorry for yesterday," he spoke to me with tears in his eyes. It took everything in my might to not spit in his lying-ass face. Instead I stayed completely still and let him spill more lies.

"I'm working on my jealousy. I know you are not cheating, and I know you love me. I'm going to prove to you that I love you, too. If you want me to leave just say the word and I'll go, but only long enough to fix this. You have to promise to let me back in and make it better."

And the reason for him leaving would be for what? So that he could come back after a week, stay straight for another, and beat the shit out of me the moment things didn't go his way? I would tell him I wanted him to leave; that would turn into another drawn-out conversation of him not believing that I would actually want him out. *Who would I find to love me like he does?* That would be his reasoning, and it would only end up turning into an argument. I lay there and said nothing because there was nothing to say. We'd already had this conversation a trillion times. Just as many times as the convo about therapy, but neither had panned out to be worthwhile so there was really no use in constantly taking about it.

He didn't say anything further either. Instead he stood and scooped me up, placed me on the toilet in the bathroom, and afterward in the tub scrubbed my naked body from head to toe like he normally did. I was placed on the bed shortly after, where he watched me like a hawk. Only this time I slid into the pajamas that he had laid out. The ritual.

At times he was as sweet as pie, and those were the times I missed. During breakfast I thought back to the first night we shared and all the nights afterward.

It was like magic, and he had me wide open. The next morning I called out from work with a fake stomach bug and we spent the morning in bed getting to know each other even further.

In the daylight he had the body of a God, and I crawled all over it for as long as he would let me. We barely made it through breakfast before the syrup became a part of foreplay and it was back popping again. A man who could cook and serve up good dick was tops in my book every time. We took the time to bathe each other after a quick nap, and went right back at again. By the time I got to work the next day I was extra tired, but both Michelle and I had so much catching up to do. Apparently she called out the day before for the same reason, and we fell out laughing as we responded to a domestic call over the radio.

When we pulled up to the house you could hear the disturbance from the street. The man was obviously drunk, and the woman was scared to death from the sound of her cries that could be heard through the door. I hated these types of calls because it could go either all the way to the left or way to the right. There was never any middle ground in these types of situations.

I climbed the few steps with Michelle at my back and knocked firmly on the door. The noise inside the house died down instantly, and all I could hear were long sobs from the woman. The door flew open moments later, and I was first greeted by the strong smell of alcohol as my eyes traveled up the body of a giant. I knew at the moment that the woman was petite. That's normally how these types of situations worked out. Michelle stepped to the side out of earshot and immediately called for backup because there was no way we could take him down ourselves if we had to.

"We got a call from your neighbors reporting a domestic violence dispute," I spoke to the guy, looking him in his drunken eyes. Well, his drunken eye . . . one swam around his socket like a loose marble and I wondered what he had to offer with a face like the one he was sporting.

"Yo, fuck all these neighbors! Fuck all these bitch-ass niggas!" he shouted, looking like he was ready to come out swinging.

"Sir, I'll need you to calm down. Who else is here with you?" I asked him as I attempted to look around his frame. He took up the entire doorway so that move was in vain.

"Why are you here? Nobody needs you here. Ain't it a doughnut shop you need to go to?" he slurred out as he nearly fell over in the door. I took a step back, placing my hand on my gun just in case I needed to blast this fool. At the very moment backup pulled up, and they piled out of the car, ready for action.

"Sir, you're drunk. I'm going to need you to step out of the house and place your hands—"

"Bitch, if you want me out, take me out."

I had to compose myself. I didn't take kindly to disrespect but it came with the job, and I knew he was going to be a handful when we pulled up on the scene. One of the male officers who pulled up on the scene approached us to take control of the situation. I was steaming and was ready to be all over his ass, but I kept my cool. Our goal was to get the other members of the family out safely. Before I could react, old drunk ass came barreling out the house toward me, and my male counterparts had to wrestle his extra-strong ass to the ground. I straight snuck one in on him for being disrespectful, but my focus was getting into the house and getting whoever was in there to safety.

Upon entry I noticed several holes in the wall and broken dishes on the floor. I was so caught up in the chaos and disarray of the house that I almost missed the woman shrunk down in the corner beside the couch. Just as I thought, she was a very petite woman, fair in complexion, sporting deep-set black eyes and a busted lip. My heart went out to her instantly, and the minute she saw me she broke down again. I didn't normally touch anyone I was here to "save" but she fell into my arms in a heap of sobs and there was nothing for me to do but hold her.

"What happened?" I asked her as I pulled up a chair and sat her down in it. She was crying so hard her body was shaking, but that didn't guarantee that she would go. I saw this same type of scenario enough times to know better.

"I had another miscarriage," she squeaked out in a soft voice. "This was the third one that he beat out of me, and he got upset that I blamed him."

"Why do you stay?" I asked her, already knowing the answer. She had that Captain Save a Ho syndrome that most women in abusive relationships get. She's trying to get things back to a better time in their lives, and she's willing to fight to her death to get it. I'd seen this situation so many times before, and I recognized it in her too.

"Because I love him. He needs me," she answered with a straight face.

I went through the motions of offering her help, and explaining that there are safe havens that she could go to that he would never find her at. I told her that there was a way out and her life was worth it. I tried to convince her that she deserved more and could do better, but she wasn't trying to hear me. He already had her brainwashed. At that very moment I vowed that I would never let a man have that much control over me. There was no way in the world that I would allow another breathing human to dictate my every move and lock down this free spirit. There was no way in the world this could happen to me.

Just as I said all I could say, and had already given her info on the national abuse hotline, I saw a movement out of the corner of my eye that caught my attention. At first I thought it might have been a cat or a small dog, but once I focused I could see a tiny pair of hands; then a small body emerged with the most beautiful eyes I'd ever seen on a child. The mother spoke to him in Spanish, and he ran into her arms, turning to look at me afterward. I felt horrible for him. If she didn't think he was reason enough to leave then what else could I say?

I left that house a little broken that night, and both Michelle and I sat in silence all the way back to the precinct, deep in thought. I didn't know what was going through Michelle's mind but mine was blown. How could you tell someone you love them with your mouth and punch them with your fist? That night when Darius came to pick me up after work I was still quiet on the ride back. When I got to the front door and he came around to open my door I broke out in tears and fell into his arms. Through tears I replayed the evening, still not able to wrap my mind around the situation at hand.

On that night he promised me forever. He said that he would never treat me that way, and that he cherished me. He dried my tears with his kisses and made the sweetest love to me over and over again until he was sure that I believed him. He swore that he would never raise his hand to me, and assured me that people who did those types of things had problems. He told me he loved me and that completely sealed the deal. I trusted him to keep his word. Unfortunately not every story ends in a "happily ever after," and it was only a matter of time before the clock struck twelve and Cinderella had to run away from the castle. In my case I didn't have evil stepsisters though. Instead I had a big bad wolf that would not let me be. I turned into that same woman I saw that night with the same issues, but the only difference was I was going to change it when the time was right. That was a promise I made to myself.

You have to understand something about my situation, although you may not agree with my reasoning. I loved Darius more than I loved myself at one point. It's painful to see someone you hold so dear to you change so drastically. In those rage-filled moments it was almost like an out-of-body experience, and I kept feeling like I could get through to him. I could love him more, I could break through that wall that he'd built, and I could get him to see the real me. I kept hoping that he would let me in, but I realized that it probably would never happen. Now it was about saving myself, and doing so as safely as possible.

7

A Change Is Gonna Come

Darius changed overnight it seemed like. In a good way, but not really. Yeah, he was less angry nowadays, and it had been awhile since he actually laid a hand on me. We even managed to have sex once or twice over the last three weeks that wasn't forced. Still, there was something with him that wasn't adding all the way up, like one plus one equaled out to three. He hadn't started the therapy sessions like he promised, but I didn't bother with him about it because I didn't want to start a chain reaction and have him start swinging on me again.

It was like we were back at the dating stage in our relationship, only instead of letting me out in front of the door he actually came in. We hung out some days after work, and were even considering trying to have a child. For Valentine's Day he actually proposed to renew our vows, and I was certain that he was ready to build the proper life for me and him. I won't lie and say what Sharla warned me of didn't keep me up many of nights because it did. She told me not to fool with him, but I had this weakness for allowing people to show me who they were instead of taking heed to warnings. Silly me for not getting out a long time ago.

One thing I noticed was that he kept his cell phone with him at all times. Before he would leave his cell phone around the house, and barely made any calls on it, but he knew that I was too afraid to touch it. There was no way I would risk being caught going through his personal business and having to face the repercussions. Besides, he never showed me any indication that there might be someone I had to compete with. That is, unless he was whipping her the way he beat me.

Lately he had his phone glued to his hip, and he was always smiling and texting, laughing out loud at whatever whoever he was talking to was texting back. One time I got up the nerve to ask him who he was chatting with, but he merely brushed me off, telling me that it was one of the guys he worked with. His eyes told me another story and I could see the lie spread across his face as he averted his eyes back to his phone. I let it go because we had just started really getting along, and I didn't want to ruin what we were trying to build with a bout of jealousy. It could just very well have been my insecurity. Maybe there was no other woman. I mean, if there was, why would he try so hard to hold on to me? That was the reasoning I stuck with, and that's what I used to allow me to sleep at night on the nights I was actually able to get a snooze or two in.

This behavior went on over the course of a few months, and it got to the point where he was just plain disrespect-ful with it. The beatings had stopped awhile back, and I was happy about that. It was actually nice to get up in the morning and not have to worry about covering a black eye, or having to lie to one of my coworkers about how I got a busted lip. Still, he was out in the streets more often than I liked, and it was a problem for me that I wasn't 100 percent sure that I wanted to put on the table. I wasn't sure if I wanted to risk getting beat again because I questioned his whereabouts.

A few nights a week after he would drop me off he told me he was just leaving to go hang out with the guys from work, but he wouldn't make it home until the wee hours of the morning, oftentimes smelling like some perfume I didn't own. When I finally got up the nerve I confronted him about it, and he said it was just the perfume the waitress wore at some random bar he was at. He had me ready to start swinging because I knew he was telling a lie, but I couldn't beat him so I just kept quiet.

It got to be overwhelming when the phone started going off during the night. I could hear the vibration through his pants pocket, but this fool slept right through it. One night the phone buzzed so many times I couldn't take it anymore. Darius had passed out in a drunken stupor hours before so I decided to go for it. I got out of the bed as quietly as I could without waking him, and when I bent down in front of the bed to get my robe, I grabbed his phone from the floor. It looked like it had slid out of his pants from the constant vibrations. Checking to be sure that he was still asleep, I slipped away into the bathroom to see who it was who was keeping me up.

The minute I locked the door I sat down and looked through his phone as quickly as I could before he realized I was gone. There wasn't too much going on, just a few text messages from his coworkers that looked innocent, and the texts that just came through asked if they were still going to the game tomorrow night. I was a little upset that I didn't even know there was a game going on, but I moved past that as I looked through his call log.

All of the numbers had names except for one, and they were all incoming calls at weird hours of the day when I wouldn't be around. Some of the calls were quick where others lasted a few minutes. None were longer than ten, but a lot can be said in that little bit of time. Committing the number to memory, I flushed the toilet and moved to wash my hands. Just as I was drying my hands a banging on the door startled me, and I felt trapped. Darius had woken up. Did he realize his phone was missing? My heart was beating a million miles an hour, and I knew I had to brace myself for the worst. I contemplated flushing the phone or sticking it in the medicine cabinet, but I wasn't even sure if the phone would go down the damn drain. My hands were shaking and I broke out in a cold sweat because I knew what was going to happen. I was about to get my ass beat. I should have just let the damn phone stay on the floor, but hopefully curiosity wouldn't kill this cat tonight. Slipping the phone into my robe pocket, I swung the door open and stooped to place the paper towel in the trash, hoping he wouldn't bang my head against the porcelain sink or against the wall.

"Hurry the fuck up. I have to piss," he said in a groggy voice as he shoved me out of the way. I scurried out of the way and was able to place his phone back in his pocket and was back in the bed before he came back into the room. I felt a little relief that I had gotten away with it, and it didn't appear that he even realized the phone was gone. I knew for sure that once I got to work I was definitely going to look into that number. If Darius had something going on I was about to find out, and then he would be handled accordingly. He stumbled in the room a few minutes later, not bothering to flush the toilet or wash his hands. When he got into the bed the silence was heavy, and I was waiting for him to fall asleep again so that I could follow suit.

"You find what you was looking for?" he asked out of nowhere. I was shocked into silence because I thought I had gotten away with it. He was asleep and I didn't think I was gone that long. I lay there in silence, not knowing if I should even try to answer.

"Did you find what you were looking for?" he asked again, this time sitting up in the bed and facing me. Before I could answer his fist came crashing into the side of my face, and I felt a ringing in my ear.

"Simone, I know you hear me. As a matter of fact let me help you."

He snatched me out of the bed and dragged me across the room. I began kicking and screaming, not caring if the neighbors heard me this time because I wanted help. I wanted out. I wanted this never-ending nightmare to finally end. His foot silenced my screams as it slammed into my chest, knocking the wind out of me. I couldn't believe I was back here again. He grabbed the phone from the floor and shoved it in my hand. I couldn't really see in the dark room but I knew what he was trying to do. He wanted to prove that he wasn't cheating on me.

"Call the number to get your answer," he demanded as he stood over me ready to strike. I was still trying to catch my breath, and a cry was trapped in my throat that I couldn't get out. He stooped down and got right in my face, and I could still smell the alcohol that made his breath smell stale.

"I . . . I don't want to call," I managed to push out in between ragged breaths. I regretted ever touching the damn phone, and this was a lesson learned that it would never happen again.

"Of course you do," he taunted. "You took the liberty of going through my personal business like you wanted to know. Well there it is, go for it."

"Darius, I don't want to call," I said again. At this point was it even worth it? I just wanted to call it a night. I really didn't want this to go as far as it did. I felt like Anna Mae telling Ike I didn't want to eat the cake.

"The next time you think it's okay to look at my personal items know that's it's not. Do we have an understanding?" he asked as he got up and got back in the bed.

"Yes," I replied, relieved that he decided to let it die for the night.

"Good. You stay on the floor and think about what you did. When you find a suitable apology let me know and we can talk further. I'm going to sleep soon so don't take long. I'm expecting you in the bed by morning."

I lay on the floor for a little while longer, thanking God that I made it through another night. I would apologize to him in the morning, but I was getting to the bottom of these phone calls whether he wanted me to or not. I didn't want to have to include people, but I knew I would need Sharla to help me with this one. I hated the fact that I even had to ask her for help because I knew she would take this opportunity to rub it in my face. At this point I really didn't even care. I took too much from Darius to be sharing him with some other chick he was probably treating better than me. I just had to chalk it up, and go to her. It was my last resort. I just had to formulate a plan so that she didn't know it was me.

Crawling into the bed, I tucked my sore body under the covers and willed myself to go to sleep because I would have to get up to report to work soon. This entire scenario was getting on my nerves, and something was about to come of this. Darius was not about to like it, but it had to be done. At this point it didn't matter, because my life depended on it and at this point I was willing to risk everything.

8

When You Least Expect It

I was beyond irked when I woke up the next morning. I couldn't believe he had the audacity to even entertain cheating on me as much as I took from him. The beatings, the lies, the bullshit . . . it all was coming to head and about to burst. I was tired of living this life, and it was time to make moves.

I went through the regular morning motions of bathing and beating my face with MAC to cover up my scars, and I engaged him in idle conversation as he drove me to work. I was a little sore in my chest from the blow last night, but the anger I was feeling amounted to much more than that so I barely felt it. When we got the station I got out of the car without saying good-bye, something that he hated, but I didn't even care. I was so beyond irked at this point, and for real if it took for me to die in the process then that would be my fate. I refused to wake up another morning sore and defeated. I didn't know what I done in a past life that made it so that I had to live this life like this but I was over it. I deserved better, I wanted better, and I was going to get it by any means necessary.

He said he didn't like us not speaking in case something happened to either of us so that there wouldn't be any guilt on not saying good-bye. If that was the case why did he beat me almost on the regular? Hell, I was hoping that today would be the day something happened to his ass so that he could leave me the hell alone.

When I got into the building the first people I saw were Sharla and Michelle. The look on my face must have said everything because Michelle instantly escorted me into the bathroom, and nosey-ass Sharla followed closely behind. I was sure that Michelle knew I had a lot going on at home, and after the first time she questioned me she respected me enough not to question me again once I told her I couldn't talk about it. I really wasn't fooling anyone, because everyone probably knew that I was getting my ass beat. I took off too many days and had too many injuries not to be, but as with our policy when dealing with domestic disputes, we couldn't make the person leave. It had to be done willingly.

"What's wrong?" my friend asked me as she handed me paper towels to wipe the tears from my eyes. Sharla stood with her back to the door, donning a smirk on her face that I was ready to knock clean off.

"Sharla, I need you to do me a favor," I responded, not even bothering to answer Michelle's question. She looked shocked at first, like she couldn't believe I was even addressing her, but shortly after the smirk returned.

"A favor? What would that be?"

"I have this number I need you to trace from my man's cell phone. I need you to tell me who it is," I went to Sharla not caring if she knew my situation at this point. At first I was embarrassed and was thinking of ways to not make it obvious that I needed help, but at this point in the game it didn't really matter.

"Simone, do you think Darius is stepping out on you?" Michelle asked me. There was so much I wanted to tell her, but now was definitely not the time. Especially with Sharla in my face at the moment.

"Can you do it or what?" I asked Sharla, again ignoring Michelle's question. I could have done the trace myself, but Sharla was very efficient and knew how to work the system without being detected. I was so fed up with this entire Darius situation, and my next move would be determined by the information I got back from Sharla. Shit was about to change, and I was about to use this good badge to my advantage. I had some things I needed to look into to make sure that if a move needed to be made I wouldn't be put in jail for it. I was covering my ass, and making sure that everything I planned to do would be justifiable.

"Okay, give me the number, and I'll see what I can come up with. What's in it for me?" she asked after plugging the number into her cell phone.

"We'll discuss it. Just know you'll definitely be taken care of."

With that said I walked out of the bathroom and waited for Michelle to join me in the squad car. When I stepped outside the building Darius was still out front and I could see the grizzly he had in his face as I walked right past my car and hopped into the passenger seat of my squad car. At this point it was like a do-or-die mission and I was ready to go out in a blaze. This shit was getting to be too much, and I had to do something to get things right. If that meant one of us had to die then so be it.

When Michelle finally got into the car she had the strangest look on her face, like she wanted to ask me a million questions. I wanted to tell her everything, but I knew I couldn't because when I did what I had to do I didn't want to drag anyone else into the mix. This was all solo, and I was going to handle it the way it needed to be handled. It wasn't until we got a few blocks down that she actually questioned me.

"Simone, you know you can talk to me. I'm worried about you. Please tell me what's going on."

"Michelle," I said to her not really knowing if I should really keep it all the way real with her, and quickly deciding against it. "I'll tell you when the time is right, okay? Now is just not the time. Can you just trust me on this?"

She was hesitant to answer. In all of the time that we'd been friends we had never kept anything major from each other. This situation was embarrassing for me. I knew if I explained it all to her she would be devastated that I hadn't told her sooner. I could have been out and been getting help. I didn't want her to look at me differently. I was grateful that she decided not to press the issue because I really didn't want to discuss it any further. I just needed that confirmation from Sharla so that I could make my next move.

"So, you're going to be an auntie," she said real nonchalant. My head whipped around toward her, and a smile spread across her face.

"I'm going to be an auntie?" I repeated to her like a parakeet. Tears came to my eyes instantly, and I reached over and hugged her, thankful we were at a red light. I cried because I was so happy for her and I mourned for the losses I endured along the way.

We were supposed to be walking hand in hand, living the life on top. We had the house with the picket fence and the men we wanted to be with, but for me the baby thing just wasn't coming into fruition the way it was supposed to. I miscarried four times. All at the hands of Darius. The first time, he pushed me down the steps because I took too long coming down the steps that morning. I had already taken a pregnancy test at work, but I wasn't going to give him a solid yes on a pregnancy until I was seen by my gynecologist.

That morning when I woke up I felt so dizzy when I sat up in the bed. We had spent most of the night arguing about some shit I couldn't quite remember. Well, he was the one at the top of his lungs in my face. I was pretty much quiet because there was no use trying to get my point across to someone who wasn't really trying to hear me. I was waiting for the opportunity to tell him that we might be expecting since I had the positive pregnancy test in my bag, but I was more so concerned with being knocked upside my head, so I had to keep my guard up for that.

I knew for Darius a plastic stick with a line in it wouldn't be enough. He would want the paper from the doctor with the ultrasound confirming that he was going to be a dad. I was hoping that having this baby would bring us closer, and maybe back to the way things used to be between us. In my mind there was no way he would lay a hand on me when I was carrying his child, and hopefully after the baby got here our love could resurface and continue to grow.

I was dragging that morning. I knew I was, but I just couldn't speed up. I knew how much Darius hated running behind, but I just didn't have the energy. I didn't know where he was in the house but at some point I finally got up the strength to slip into my uniform and get ready for the day. I won't lie to you; I spent a lot of time that morning wondering what my baby would look like. When I turned sideways in the mirror, I tried to picture my belly getting round, and knew I would have to be put on desk duty because I couldn't be in the field with a pregnant belly. I could only imagine the baby shower they would give me, and that would also be a reason for my family to come back around again.

I actually had a smile on my face as I went to leave my room. Things were going to be great, and I felt good about everything that was happening. As I approached the top of the staircase Darius appeared out of nowhere, coming up behind me. I grabbed the banister so that I wouldn't trip, but before I could even get my footing he shoved me from behind. I tried to grab at anything I could but there was nothing but air as my body lurched forward and I connected with the steps, stumbling down before rolling in a ball and landing at the bottom.

I could hear his heavy footsteps as he took his time coming toward me. I was lying on the bottom of the staircase wedged between the wall and a small desk. Holding my stomach I began to cry in shock. What if he killed my baby?

"How many times did I have to tell you to hurry up?" he asked me as he placed his foot into my abdomen and pressed down, almost coming into a full stand on my stomach. The pain was sharp and hot, and it felt like my organs were going to burst open. I could feel a lot of heat between my legs; it felt like I was actually peeing on myself.

"Answer my question," he demanded as he pressed harder.

"Darius, I think . . ." I managed to get out right before I blacked out.

When I came to I was in the back of an ambulance with a mask over my face, and I could hear Darius tell the EMT that I slipped and fell down the stairs. I started clawing at my stomach, hoping that my child had been spared. I wanted to ask the man if he could hear a heartbeat in my belly but I couldn't form any words. I started swinging, but whatever they gave me knocked me back out again.

The next time I woke up I was in a room in the emergency department, but Darius was nowhere in sight. I had an IV in my arm, and I was hooked up to a breathing machine. I managed to find the pager for the nurse, and when I pressed the button she came in right away with the doctor.

"Where is my husband?" I asked the doctor. He had a real solemn look on his face, and I made me wonder if Darius had got locked up.

"He just stepped out to get a drink," he said to me before taking a look in my chart. "I'm glad to see that you are up finally. How are you feeling?"

"I'm groggy and in pain."

"Yeah, you are going to feel a little groggy from the pain meds you were given. I'm not sure if you were aware, but you were pregnant when you came in. Your husband said you fell down the stairs, but you must have hit your stomach during the fall. In any event, you miscarried. Now I know this may be hard for you, but . . ."

I couldn't hear anything else he said after that. Pulling the sheet back, I hiked my hospital gown up to get a look at my stomach. I lost my baby. I lost my baby! I wanted to die at that moment, and all I could do was curl into a ball in cry. At some point I heard the doctor talking to someone else, and once I heard Darius respond I wanted to cry even harder. He killed my baby. When the doctor left the room Darius came to the side of my bed and sat down. I hated him so much at that moment, and I just wanted him to go. I didn't care where he went; I just didn't want him here anymore.

"Simone, I'm sorry this happened to you. I didn't know. You know how I hate to be late, I was just . . . I'm sorry."

I didn't say a word. At that point there was no way in the world he could hurt me more than I was at that moment. Sobs racked my body as I mourned the loss of my first child. Everything that I had envisioned was gone in a blink of an eye. I knew I deserved better, and I needed Darius to understand that.

"Simone, we can try for another one. I didn't know . . . Please don't leave me; let me make this up to you."

To this day I still didn't know why I stayed, but I did. Well, let me not lie. I did know. I stayed because I believed in us. I stayed because I knew with my whole heart that a baby would bring us back to where we needed to be. It would restore our unity, and we would be happy again. I stayed because it was the right thing to do in my head. A moment I'd been regretting more and more.

I wanted to share this with my friend, but I just didn't have the strength or the energy to even relive the tragedy. I could see the happiness and I beamed with joy for her and the love that she managed to find. I was truly happy for her and I told her just that.

"I would like for you and Darius to be the godparents," she said as she drove along.

"Absolutely," I responded, allowing her to chat away about her new venture. If I could help it Darius wouldn't even make the birth of the baby. I had a plan, and I was ready to put it into motion.

9

Too Many Times to Count

It took Sharla a lot longer than I thought it would to get back to me with the information about the number I gave to her. A part of me thought that she was just making me suffer since she was obviously still mad about me snagging Darius before her. Little did she know she wasn't missing out on a damn thing. Come to find out this fool was a damn lunatic with a hand problem. A part of me also believed that Sharla probably wouldn't have put up with it for as long as I had.

In the following months, Darius's attitude was at either extreme. He was either happy or pissed way the fuck off. Nothing ever really fell in between . . . the usual for Darius. He felt like shit for a little while after the miscarriage, but not bad enough not to beat the second baby out of me. I was at such a loss, and once Michelle was put on desk duty because of her growing belly and I ended up partnering with one of the guys in the squad, that only turned up the heat on the home front even more.

"So you telling that out of all the females in there you have to sit next to this dude all day?" he questioned for the millionth time as I got dressed to get ready for work. We had already been over this, and I didn't know how many more ways I could explain that I could not pick who my partner was.

"Darius, everyone is already paired up. My partner is on desk duty because she's pregnant. You know that already. I'm floating until she comes back."

"I see a lot of girl cops up in there. Why can't you work with any of them?" he asked, sounding like a child having a tantrum because he wasn't getting his way.

"I have worked with them, Darius. I just worked with Monica two days ago. Jesus . . ."

He was on my ass in no time. I had to catch myself because I didn't even realize that he had his hands around my neck choking the life out of me until I went to take my next breath. He was way stronger than me, and it seemed like no matter how hard I clawed at his hands he just wouldn't let go. I could feel my eyes rolling into the back of my head and my lungs began to feel tight. *This must be how it feels to drown.* Just at the brink of blacking out he let me go and I crumbled to the floor. As I gasped for air he went and took his seat back on the bed like it was nothing and continued to throw questions at me like I hadn't already answered.

"You better not be fucking none of them dudes." He glared at me like he hated my very existence. "Now, hurry up and put your makeup on before you are late for work. I'll be downstairs so don't take forever."

I waited for him to leave before I struggled from the floor, taking a seat on the ottoman at the end of the bed. This man was going to kill me, I knew it. I had to get with Sharla the minute I got to work because this was truly getting old. Right now I was supposed to be ecstatic about planning my best friend's surprise baby shower, but all I could think about was putting my husband out of his misery.

I was hoping it wouldn't have to come to this, but I knew what I had to do. A few years ago I purchased a small handgun that I carried in a secret compartment in my purse. It had an invisible zipper in the bottom of my bag, and I kept tons of shit in my bag to camouflage the fact that it was in there. Gun laws prohibit people carrying loaded weapons even if it is registered to you, but I kept one in the chamber and the safety on at all times because I knew when it came time to use it I would have to act fast and would not have time to put bullets in. I would need to pull it out, remove the safety, and shoot.

When I got to the living room Darius was sitting on the edge of the couch, looking at the news. He still looked beyond pissed off, and truth be told my face matched his. I was pissed off to the max, and I wished I had an older brother or somebody who lived close. I wanted his ass beat for every blow that ever landed on me, for all of the children I lost, and all the sleepless nights in between.

I stopped long enough to grab my bag from the couch, and as I was walking past him I resisted the urge to spit in his face. I resented this man. I hated him and I wanted him dead. He tried to bust it up during the drive like nothing ever happened, and I kept my face straight and my mouth shut the entire ride. We didn't have shit to talk about, and I meant it.

When I got to the job I saw Sharla going into the building so I hurried up out of the car so that I could catch up with her before the morning meeting. I needed that info now. When I got into the building she was standing by Michelle's desk chatting, and I wasted no time walking right up on her in mid conversation.

"Did you forget what I asked you to do?" I barked at her, no good morning or anything.

"Yeah, I got what you asked for weeks ago. I've just been busy," she said with a smirk. I almost jumped on her ass, but I remembered that I needed something from her.

"Well where is it?"

"It's right here. I was actually just about to put it on your desk." She smirked in my face. She held up a brown manila envelope that looked thick. It made me wonder if it was full of some bullshit, but Sharla was known for being very accurate with her information, and I knew that the contents of that envelope were going to change my life forever.

"I hate to be the one to say I told you so . . . but no, really," she taunted me, followed up with a slight laugh. "Everything you need to know is here, so don't be a fool with this information. It appears that you need this more than I thought so this one is on me. Don't say I've never done anything for you."

Placing the envelope in my hands, she bade her good-byes to Michelle and switched off, afterward having a jovial conversation with one of the male officers who was on duty that morning. Michelle looked at me like she wanted to ask me what was going on, and I could see that she struggled to stay in her lane. When you love someone it's hard to turn a blind eye, but it was better that she stayed out of this. The fewer witnesses I had the better.

"I promise I will tell you when it's all said and done. Please just trust me on this," I said to her as I blinked back tears. Her tears flowed freely, and I could tell that it was killing her not to say anything to anyone.

"I love you, Simone. Please be careful."

"I will. I love you too."

I walked away from her and into the bathroom so that I could see what Sharla had dug up. I was ready to end it all, and I knew that once I opened that envelope there was no turning back. Going into the last stall, I took a seat and pulled back the tabs on the envelope. Taking a deep breath I started to pull the contents out one by one, and I couldn't believe what I was seeing.

The first thing I pulled out was a call log from his cell phone. Darius was having extensive conversations that sometimes lasted for an hour or more, when in the beginning there were conversations only for a few minutes here and there. Next out was a log of text messages to this mystery person. He told her constantly that he loved her, and that as soon as his divorce was final they could be together. He even told her in one text that he was just waiting for the right time to break it to our kids that he was leaving. We didn't have any children! My mouth was wide open as I read all the lies and deception that went on for pages at a time. A few of the text messages were at time when we were together. A pure mess if I'd ever seen one.

Reaching back into the envelope, I was floored. The woman in this picture was a fellow officer from another district. I remembered seeing her at a few galas, and we sometimes did the same events when a mass call was in order to control the crowd. I remembered seeing her in plenty of places, and she knew that me and Darius were a couple.

Each photo was worse than the one before. They were hugged up and kissing, holding hands in public, and there were even shots of her driving my car. The farther I flipped through the more intimate the pictures got. There were photos of them having sex in a room that I didn't recognize, and he was doing shit to her that he had never done to me. I was livid, but I had to follow the plan. Darius was going to pay for everything he'd ever done to me.

As I tried to stuff the items back into the envelope, a smaller envelope was at the bottom. Pulling it out, I opened it to find more pictures. These were of women who were abused. They had black eyes, busted lips, missing teeth, and broken bones. There were photos of three women. On the back of the pictures were the names and the time frame that they were in a relationship with Darius. Two of the women had relocated into a safe shelter and one of the women was dead. At the moment I knew there was no turning back. I had to move forward with the plan, and I had to make things right.

Taking the evidence that Sharla got for me, I stuck it in my locker for safe keeping because I didn't want to chance taking it home and Darius finding it. I was going to have to catch him slipping and at his most vulnerable moment. I was going to have to make it look like I was defending myself, or make it look like an accident. Either way, what I had to do was going to be permanent.

On the way out I stopped past Michelle's desk and gave her a hug, assuring her that I was okay, and that I was cool. One day I was going to sit down and tell her everything, and I just hoped that it wouldn't be from behind bars.

10

After the Love Is Gone

Does he threaten to hurt you, your kids, or a family pet? Does he make you ask for money? Does he threaten to harm himself if you try to leave? Does he make you stay in the house until he gets home? Does he treat you like a child?

Michelle's baby shower came around faster than any of us anticipated. Even more so because Michelle ended up having the baby a month earlier than expected. It was all good to us because her baby shower just turned into a welcoming party for her and her husband's bundle of joy. Darius and I showed up of course, this after an argument that lasted for days and ended up putting me in the hospital.

The day that I got home after Sharla gave me the information I needed, Darius was unusually quiet on the way home. There wasn't even any idol conversation at red lights like usual. I was expecting an argument in the driveway, or even a fight once we got inside, but surprisingly it was the total opposite. He had dinner done, and flowers for me in a vase on the table. I wasn't impressed at all. This was the same makeup scene from the last million or so times, and I couldn't help but think if he did this kind of shit with the bitch he was cheating on me with.

"Are you seeing someone else?" I asked him, not really

expecting a straight answer. Darius lied about a lot of shit, come to find out, and I knew this time wouldn't be any different.

"Of course not. Why would I cheat on you?" he asked me with a bewildered look on his face like he couldn't believe I would think such a thing about him.

"That's what I'm trying to figure out."

"There's nothing to figure out. So let's just get through dinner."

Of course he denied having a mistress when I asked him about it, and since I decided against showing him the pictures I didn't have any valid proof that he was dogging me out. We went back and forth about it for a while, and he ended up punching me in the face and breaking my nose.

We showed up to Michelle's party all smiles, but my body was so sore and I just wanted to go home. Her baby was gorgeous, and it was so painful to look at her. A few times throughout the night I was able to avoid my turn when the baby was passed to me, but Darius was watching me like a hawk and already threatened me about being sensitive.

"Haven't you embarrassed me enough? I mean, how hard is it to keep a baby in ya pussy?" he asked me one night after unfulfilling sex. "We actually have to show up at a party to fucking celebrate some other bitch's baby, and we don't have shit of our own. What the fuck is we even together for?"

Speechless. He straight caught me off-guard with that one and it cut deep. I couldn't believe that he didn't think he was the reason why I wasn't pregnant after all this time. He took life from me . . . repeatedly Was this fool serious?

"Darius, you can't expect me to—"

"I can't expect you to do shit right. I already know that.

You a simple bitch."

I tried my damnedest to hold my tears in. This man was just so insensitive. It made me wonder how I ever loved him in the first place. He was nothing like the man I met, and I rewound my life a few times to see if I missed any flags and flashing red lights before shit started to get real bad. Yeah, he had a temper on him, but so did I. He eventually beat mine out of me though.

Does he go into drunken fits? Does he blame you for his indiscretions? Does he promise to stop the violence only to do it again? Does he beat you in front of your children? Is he different around family members?

"Why would you think that I would purposely not want to have your baby, Darius? How does that sound?" I asked him in a desperate attempt to make sense of the situation. My mother and father had a loving relationship, and I never heard my dad so much as raise his voice at my mom in front of us. He was an example of the type of man I was supposed to be with. Where did I go wrong?

"So you saying it's my fault? I'm the reason why I'm not a father right now?"

"Did you forget the trip down the steps and you standing up into my stomach? Or what about the time you punched me in my gut because I was taking too long coming out of a meeting with my boss? Did I do all of those things to myself?"

Silence. It filled the room louder than the loudest sound in the world. We both stayed completely still. I wasn't sure about what was going on in his head, but I refused to take the blame when I wasn't at fault. Sometimes silence can be so loud and it was to the point when it was deafening. It felt like an out-of-body experience, and at that moment I felt like I shouldn't have said anything. Then again the truth had to be told, so it was kind of a "damned if you do, damned if you don't" situation.

Boom! The sound of his fist crashing against the side

of my face was louder than the silence. I started swinging out of instinct . . . out of desperation . . . out of fear. I couldn't go out like this, and if this was the way I was going to go then I was going out fighting. I had nothing to lose at this point, and I was fully ready to accept my fate if he killed me. Anything would be better than continuing to live in this hell.

I somehow rolled off the bed and landed somewhere between the nightstand and the bed frame. When Darius rounded the bed to my side I just started kicking, not caring where my feet landed. I was hoping that I was kicking him in his balls. I didn't want him to ever be able to stick his raggedy dick in anyone else again. Not even me.

He managed to grab my by the collar of my nightgown and drag from out of the wedge I was in. With me being in such a tight space it was hard for him to really get a hit in without me kicking the shit out of him, so I guess he had to even the playing field. He dragged me across the room, and banged my body against the wall. I started swinging again because my life depended on it. It felt like we was fighting forever, and I refused to let up. *I'm not going out without a fight.*

"You a simple bitch. I'm out of this joint," he screamed at me right before storming out of the room.

I didn't have the energy to make him stay. I was battered . . . I was bruised . . . I was done. As far as I was concerned he could get hit by a fast-moving train at this point and I wouldn't even show up at his funeral. Fuck him.

Stretching out on the floor on my back I wished for a second that a fast-moving train would take me too. Life had to be better than this. I wasn't sure how long I was lying there or even when I fell asleep, but when I felt Darius scooping my body from the floor I started swinging on his ass again. He had to actually hold me down and tire me out before I stopped going off. I didn't think I had any more fight left in me, and at this point I was giving up. It didn't matter what happened after this.

"Simone, we're going to make this work. You have to stop fighting me, baby. I love you. We have to get past this."

I didn't say a word. I just balled up on the bed and cried myself back to sleep. I always wondered why people stayed in abusive relationships. Over the years of showing up at houses and seeing battered women and their kids, I would always question why they chose to stay and I finally got my answer. There was only one way out. Most women were probably scared to take that route, but I wasn't. I was ready to stand up and take back my life.

Does he hold you hostage? Does he threaten to end his life? Does he promise to get help? Does he abuse you then want to have sex? Does he make you look like you're the one with the problem? We'll keep asking until the violence stops. . . .

11

The Last Chance for Last Chances

Thinking back to that night I knew the decision I made was the right one. At Michelle's baby shower we showed up with plastic smiles on our faces, faking and frauding like we were a happy couple. It was mostly a blur. We laughed and Darius drank. He pretty much stayed on one side of the room with the guys, and the ladies and I sat on the other side passing the baby around. Sharla had a look of disdain on her face like she couldn't believe I even showed up with him on my arm after all the work she put in to prove he wasn't shit. I couldn't even look her in the eye because I knew she was right, but just like they tell people in those abuse classes . . . it's a process and I was seeing the light better every day.

It was almost my turn to hold the baby again so I jumped up to grab a glass of punch from the kitchen area. This shit was painful . . . so painful that it was getting hard to breathe. I wanted to leave, but Darius had the keys so I was stuck until he was ready to blow this joint. That probably meant that we wouldn't be leaving until almost all the liquor was gone.

As I started ahead I realized how out of place we were here . . . how out of place he was in this place. The room was full of law enforcement officers, both male and female, and even a few judges we were cool with. Everyone was in a position of power, and then there was Darius: a sometimes-working, hard-for-him-to-keep-a-job, abusive-ass construction worker. He was so beneath me. I could have had any man in this room I wanted, and plenty of them were checking for me. I would have a man who was on the same level as me, who could protect me. I could be living the dream . . . but all I had was Darius. That shit sucked.

"See something you like?" he asked, sneaking up behind me. He had a grip on my sore side from the spat the night before that still had my head pounding.

"Darius, I was just getting something to drink," I responded, refusing to flinch in front of all these people. I refused to put my business out there for the world to see until I was ready. On some real shit, most of them probably already knew and just chose not to say anything.

"That's your ass when we get home."

He walked away and I took a deep breath. I was so not in the mood for this shit again. Not after last night. Hopefully this fool would get drunk enough to forget and pass out when we got home. Just my luck, probably not.

We pulled up out of the party earlier than expected, and I could see the pleading look in Michelle's eyes for me to open up to her. She gave me the longest hug before we left there like it would be her last time seeing me. Maybe she knew something I didn't, but something about tonight felt different. Like it was not going to end the way I expected.

The ride home was kind of spooky; I was waiting for him to bust out swinging because I was planning to go in. We would both be dead in a car crash this time around because I wasn't taking it no more. Surprisingly we made it all the way to the door unscathed. I was preparing to get out of the car when this fool made me give him a blow job right outside. I was so fucking embarrassed, and I hoped that it would be quick. I couldn't believe this shit happened.

Even after that and I made it into the house I thought for sure that I was going to make it to the morning unscathed. I got undressed and in the bed ready to go just how he liked it. Why did I fall asleep? I knew why now. Because I was tired of dodging and ducking and running for my life. I wanted a good night's sleep and for once I wanted some peace.

This man walked on clouds. He had to because I didn't even peep what was going on until I was being dragged out of the bed once again by this maniac. *What the hell did I do this time?* He slammed me against the wall and struck me repeatedly with a closed fist. I could feel my hair being ripped from the scalp, and the blood the trickled from the gash in my head blinded my one eye as I tried to get focused on his position in the room.

"So you're in an abusive relationship? Is that what this is?"

He punched me again and I went reeling around in a circle before landing on the floor and bumping my head on the side of the dresser. I was hit with a barrage of punches to the face and chest, and even being curled up didn't soften the blows. A size thirteen Timberland boot crashed down into my rib cage, and a torn "Women Against Abuse" packet fell around me like confetti. *So this is what all of this is about.*

"Darius, let me explain . . ." I said through a bloody mouth.

"Explain what? That you're being abused? You haven't seen abused yet."

This went on for what felt like forever.

Kicking.

Punching.

Pulling.

Scratching.

Cursing.

My body went numb, and at some point I was dazed. It didn't matter. Tonight was the night I would get payback, and I wasn't going to hesitate. Darius would not get to do this to anyone else. Not if I had anything to do with it.

"Let me help you up," he said to me in a soothing voice. It was funny how he went from one extreme to the next. "I'm sorry I had to do this to you. You get me so jealous."

I managed to get myself up from the floor, and I tiptoed over to the bed to get my life. I had to do something, and who knew the opportunity to change things would be handed right to me? I wanted to know why he was even in my pocketbook to be able to find the little card-sized pamphlet, but he was sure to have some asinine reason so there was no need asking for justification. Besides, I wasn't going to ask for forgiveness for what I was about to do.

"Do you need anything? Some water? What do you need me to do? I'll have some bathwater ready for you in a moment." He fussed over me like he really gave a fuck about me.

"I just need my pocketbook. Can you just get it for me?" I spoke in a low tone. My chest and my head hurt too bad to speak up any louder, and I was hoping I would have enough strength to pull off what I was about to do. This was like the be-all and end-all for me, and it was my only option.

He came back to me with my pocketbook, and I scooted back on the bed far enough to have room to put it in my lap. I was working with sight out of only one eye so I used what little vision I had to assist with moving things around in my bag until I found the invisible zipper at the bottom of my bag. My fingers traced the smooth edge where the zipper lay flush against the side of the bag. It was amazing that out of all the times he looked and felt around in my bag he never ran across it. I pulled the zipper back, and the handle felt cool to the touch. I tucked my head into my chest a little farther to appear like I was really searching for something, and I could see that he was getting restless.

"What are you looking for?" he asked, leaning his body against the dresser and folding both his arms across his chest, and his feet crossed at the ankles.

"Some pain medicine," was my response as I clicked the safety back on the gun. This next moment was going to change my life, but I was ready for a change. I deserved it.

"Well, how long are you going to look for them? Pull the shit out."

I looked up at him and tried to remember why I fell in love with him in the first place. The room didn't go dim like it did the night at the club, and I couldn't see the little hearts floating in the air as our eyes connected. My heart was not skipping a beat because I was madly in love, and all I could see was hate. I despised him. I hated his very existence. I wanted him dead.

Slowly I pulled my hand from the bag with my finger on the trigger. Blood continued to run into my eye that was nearly swollen shut, but it didn't matter because I could hit a target dead-on with my eyes closed. The look on his face was priceless because he probably didn't think it would ever come to this.

All I could hear was the clock ticking in the bathroom accompanied by the hum of the ceiling fan going above my head. I looked at the DVR and I saw that it was a new day. The day we vowed to love each other for better or worse, through sickness and heath until death did us part. Our anniversary.

The gun was finally at eye level and I had a straight shot. He looked like a deer caught in headlights . . . just as I expected. A small smile tugged at the corner of my swollen mouth as I spoke my last words to him. This was the end. I won.

"Happy anniversary." I smiled at him, and immediately pulled the trigger. The bullet whizzed across the room and landed right between his eyes. The back of his head exploded against the wall, and his body took a slow descent toward the floor, landing in a heavy heap.

I lay back on the bed and closed my eyes. I was finally free. Every woman who had him was finally free, and any woman who was going to have him in the future could thank me later. I rummaged around my bag while still lying on my back until I found my cell phone. I lay there for ten more minutes before I finally placed the call. I had a smile on my face. A huge one . . . and I have never felt better in my life.

"9-1-1 operator. How may I direct this call?"

"There's a dead body in my house and I think you should come get it."

I didn't bother to give any more information because I knew they could trace the call. I pulled my battered and beaten body up into my bed and curled up under the covers because I was a little chilly in the room. Just as I was dozing off I could hear the sound of sirens and the police approaching my house. I took those last few minutes to find suitable clothes to put on, stopping to kick Darius's dead body in the face with my boots on. That was for every black eye, busted lip, patch of hair, broken arm, and for the children he ripped from my gut. It was over. Finally, it was over.

When the cops came I didn't even bother to put up a fight. A few of the guys who showed up were at Michelle's house for the baby shower, and couldn't believe what they were seeing. I was as cool as a cucumber as they entered the house. Michelle took me into her arms as they read me my rights and placed the cuffs on me. I was smiling wide the entire time. It didn't matter what they did to me at this point. They could lock me up and throw away the key. I didn't care. I was finally free.

Part Two

Te'Nae and Malcolm

—Jazmine Sullivan, "Redemption"

12

Road Trippin'

"So, she finally got tired of his ass, huh?" I said to myself, more as a statement than a question. My neighbor from across the street must have finally gotten fed up with that no-good man of hers. He looked like a sneaky little bastard anyway. Much like the one I was stuck living with now. What confused me was that she's a cop, but a badge don't mean a damn thing when a man is beating your ass. Hell, if it were me I would have shot his behind a long time ago. Damn the jokes. I knew shit had hit the fan when the bloodstained body bag was brought out, and once I saw her following up in handcuffs. It was none of my business though, so I simply shut my shades and kept it moving.

"One . . . two . . . three . . ."

I counted out ten Vicodin, and placed them in the shape of a heart on my kitchen table next to the bottle of Hennessy I'd been sipping from throughout the day. After keeping house and making sure the kids were asleep at my sister's house, I was finally able to sit down and have a moment to myself.

Now, before you start judging me, I'd taken a lot from Malcolm over the years and I was just tired. Tired of him coming in here all hours of the night, or not at all, like that was an okay thing to do. I was tired of him calling me out my name, and making me feel insignificant. No matter what I did around here it was never right and I was just plain old tired of this shit.

I kept the most immaculate house on the block, and I knew this because I'd visited a few of my neighbors' houses, and in a few of them I wouldn't have even drunk a glass of water out of a cup that I brought in with me, that's how nasty it was. You could eat off the damn floor in my kitchen, but of course my trifling-ass husband didn't notice that. There wasn't an ounce of dust floating in this camp because I took care to make sure that all of the filters in the central air unit stayed clean, and I wet dusted so particles wouldn't go flying around. Did this lazy nigga notice it? Hell no!

Tapping a cigarette out of a fresh pack of Newport Lights, I chanced a look at the clock. Seeing that it was later than I thought I decided that if I was going to get on the road I needed to do so within the next few hours if I was going to make it to Maryland in time enough to beat morning traffic. I was actually about to head out, but when I saw the cops roll up I had to pause for a second. Shit, I thought they were coming here, and that would have spelled a world of trouble for me.

There was no way to explain why my husband's body was chopped up into about six pieces and bagged up in industrial-type trash bags in the trunk of my truck that was parked in plain sight in the driveway. I even took the care to triple up on the bags so that the blood wouldn't stain the inside of the trunk. I didn't want to have to explain that to the police so I decided to wait until all the noise died down across the street. The minute they were gone I would be gone because I had deliveries to make.

I feel like you're already judging me, so I'll take the time to explain myself while I'm driving since all I have is time right now anyway.

I just needed to get my bags, clean up this mess I made in the kitchen, and then I would be on my way. Satisfied that the house was in order I went to the basement to make sure that there was no sign of a murder here either. It took me forever to saw through his bones, and that got to be a little messy. I made sure to clean up every drop of blood though because I didn't need my house to smell like those meat stores down Ninth and Washington. That, and once the cops started piecing shit together I didn't want all of his evidence to be right in the damn basement. Hell, I had to make it to North Carolina before all of this was said and done, and then it could be whatever after that. My kids were with family, so they would be safe. I made sure of that. My sister also had access to all of the money I had in my accounts and she was beneficiary so there wouldn't be an issue there either. I knew where this was going to end up, and I was well prepared. My family will have to find out on a need-to-know basis.

I turned off all of the lights in the house once the cops was gone, and after loading my bags and my lunch cooler in the car I checked my reflection in the mirror just outside of the living room by the door. The adult diaper I had on made me look a little bulky in the midsection area, but I didn't want to have to stop to use the restroom often so this seemed like the perfect idea. I would just stop to change it periodically when I absolutely needed to put gas in my truck. Yeah, you think I'm crazy, but until you've been through what I'd been through, who the fuck are you to judge me? Judge ya mom, and fuck that bitch, too. Your opinion don't mean shit to me at this point so for real you can go kick rocks in a pair of open-toe sandals for all I care.

Now, as I was saying, I scoped the block to make sure all signs of the law were out of sight before I pulled out. This in itself was about to be a journey, but it was necessary that I take it. I needed to purge and I needed a clear conscience because surely after this they were going to fry my black ass. It didn't matter though. No one was going to have Malcolm if I couldn't have him, and that's why I did to him what I did. How did I manage to kill him, you might ask? Well, I'll get to that later. Right now, let me just catch you up to speed.

Malcolm and I met when we were in high school, but I'm not even going to go that far back and bore you with the details. Fast forward, after college we decided to get married right around the time that I found out I was pregnant with our first child, Tamika, who is six years old now. I knew that Malcolm was a ladies' man, and I also knew he married me because it was the right thing to do since I was pregnant with his kid. Yeah, we loved each other, but I doubted very seriously that we were in love. I mean, I wasn't, but I knew I would need help taking care of the baby that would be showing its face in about six more months.

It didn't hurt that the dick was good either. Malcolm had that make-your-toes-curl, call-out-for-Jesus-and-the-Virgin-Mary, smack-him-then-smack-yourself kind of dick. That bitch had a hook in it that tapped the hell out of my spot and made me squirt all over the damn place. He was a nasty, talking-shit-in-your-ear, slap-you-on-the-ass type of dude and I loved that shit. Not him, but the beat down he gave this pussy on a regular basis, so I stayed.

We were rolling the first two years after marriage. We were happy, and we had a good life. Our house was the shit with all of the newest gadgets, and our daughter didn't want for anything. We had our date nights, and often entertained company during the warmer months. A few times I caught Malcolm having a lusty conversation with the women in the neighborhood, but it wasn't nothing to me. He was a flirt, but he never came home late, all the bills were paid on time, and I got what I wanted for both my daughter and me. The best of everything. Top-of-the-line shit, nothing but the best for me.

All of that changed when two years after that I popped up pregnant with our second kid, Talia. Oh, he straight flipped the entire script on a sista. All of a sudden I was trying to trap him, and why didn't I make sure I was on birth control? Never mind that this fool didn't bother to pull out not one time, and more often than not he knew I forgot to take the damn pills because I was always in a rush. He wasn't the only one bringing home the bacon, and with working a few hours doing the morning weather for my local news station, and making sure that Tamika made it dance class, choir practice, I still had to maintain the house. This man wanted a hot meal on the table every night. Who in hell had time to remember to take a pill every day?

At any rate, I popped up pregnant with baby number two. Now, I was on my way to take a trip across the river to lie up on a table and get it sucked out before I could get attached but this man begged me to keep it. He didn't believe in abortions, and he wanted to give the life in me a chance. That was the conversation we had the night the pink line on the pregnancy test confirmed the reason for my missed period. The very next morning everything switched up.

Malcolm had an entire attitude when we woke up that day, and on some real shit so did I. Hell, I already had my $300 counted out just in case my insurance wasn't accepted, and I had one of my girlfriends on speed dial to take the ride so that I could get it popping and keep it moving. At the end of the day he was my husband though, and he said he was cool with the situation so I was going to roll with it. It wasn't until I started showing that I wished I had followed my first instinct. The very first night he didn't come home for dinner on time, I could smell another woman on him. He pissed me right off, but at this point I was stuck. He had me where he wanted me, but I wasn't about to make this shit easy. Nope, not at all.

13

Meet the Mistress

"Where were you? I've been waiting for you to come in for hours." I questioned Malcolm from the kitchen table. My stomach was a perfectly round basketball that made it hard to move as fast as I wanted to. I was waiting for him to lie because I knew there was another woman in the picture. We always know. I just couldn't prove it at the moment.

"My meeting ran over, Te'Nae. I was going to call, but my cell phone has been dead for hours."

He said all of this without looking at me. A sure sign that he was definitely lying. I hated him at that moment because I didn't feel like having to be the troublesome baby mom from hell, but I would be. Oh believe I would act right the fuck up in the blink of an eye. I never had to go in on him before, but he really didn't want it from me. I promise you he didn't, and I hoped for his sake that he knew that much.

"Yeah, that's what happened?" I asked, seemingly uninterested as I scooted the chair back from the table, and grabbed my bottle of water. I was too tired to even go through the motions with him, but I needed him to see me in plain light before we went to sleep that night. I could already see this was going to be a problem, so it was time for me to start stacking up so when it was time to bounce I could do so and still live comfortably.

See, I wasn't one of those delusional bitches who knew the truth but ignored the red flags to make shit work. We all know it never does unless both parties want that. I was practical, and I clearly saw the signs. Now it was time to get my situation in order. At the time I didn't think it would take me four years to come up with this plan, but I never would have thought that I would even have to take it here to begin with. Either way, this was the situation, but we'll relive that at a later date.

"What? You don't believe me?" he asked, looking at me with these guilty-ass eyes. I stared him right down so that he could see that I knew the deal.

"What's not to believe? You said that your meeting ran late and your phone died hours ago. You traveled all the way from Maryland with a dead phone? Cool. No worries here. I'm going to call it a night. If you're hungry dinner is in the fridge."

With that said I wobbled my pregnant body up the steps and into our bedroom, changing into the ugliest pajamas I had once I got there. I didn't have time to entertain the shenanigans with him. I had to be at the news station by three-thirty in the morning. It was all good though. I was going to play this thing to the end, and I would definitely have the last laugh.

He crawled into the bed an hour later, but he stayed on his side of the bed. He usually did that when guilt set in, but I wasn't about to make him feel better about fucking another bitch. I hoped the guilt shredded his very soul and kept his ass up all night long. Whoever she was had better have been worth it because by the time she got him he was going to be broken down and used up before I let his ass go. Trust me.

There wasn't a whole bunch of drama on my part though. After that night he straightened up for the most part, and pretty soon things were back to normal, kind of. He never missed dinner if he was in town, and the nights he was not he called to let me know he had made it safely to the hotel. That was all well and good, but my belly was steadily growing, and pretty soon it was time for the baby to make its entrance into the world.

Just as I was pushing little Talia into the world Malcolm busted until the delivery room, gowned up just in time to see his second daughter slide out. Well, I thought it was his second daughter. Didn't find out until two years after her birth that she was actually daughter number three, and the middle child was born six months before. And where did she live? You guessed it! In Maryland. This man had more shit with him than a manure farm.

I was making pretty good time on I-95 being that most people were asleep and not on the road this time of day. It was just me and a few truck drivers eating asphalt, and it was actually kind of peaceful. I always liked this time of night. It gave me plenty of time to think being that most nights my husband wasn't there. Glen Burnie was really a hop, skip, and a jump from Philly, and where I needed to be wouldn't take long to find.

The day I decided to kill his ass kind of came as a surprise to me, but we'll have more time to discuss that in the future. For right now, let me walk you through my life. Let me tell the story while I still have time to give you my version of what happened. I mean, if that's cool with you.

So, at any rate, I now had two kids to raise, and an absentee husband. He was there for the important stuff like the first day of pre-K for Tamika, and he even dropped Talia off in the morning at day care since I had to be to work so early in the day. He was home for dinner, and made sure that he engaged our daughters in conversation. He even acted like we were still in love in front of them, but our bedroom was as dry as a bone and I was not feeling that shit.

When he came to the room he stayed on his side and I stayed on mine. The few times we did meet in the middle it was the worst. Not sure what happened to Mr. Toe Curler, but his replacement could hit the damn road. I was not feeling him, and he didn't put me in the mood. Ever. And this night was no exception.

"So you giving me some action tonight?" he asked once he came into the bedroom after putting the kids to sleep and making sure that the house was secure for the night.

"Really?"

"Yeah. Let me play with your nipples or something. Damn, since when did I have to beg for pussy that's mines?"

"When you started giving dick that's mine to other bitches."

Silence. The salt on his face said it all. At this point I didn't have full confirmation that there was anyone else. It was just a "guess-timate." I was trying to see if he was dumb enough to slip and confirm my suspicions, but Malcolm was smooth and it would take more than a slick question to catch him slipping.

"No problem. I ain't feel like sucking on no ashy nipple anyway. Keep it. I'm going to sleep."

I wanted to laugh, but I decided to let him live. He was irked to the max with me, but when you tried to play me this is what you got. He was definitely stepping out on me, and I wasn't the type of chick who was okay with sharing my dick. It was all or nothing, and that's exactly what his ass got . . . nothing. Maybe one of these days his simple ass would figure it out. In the meantime I had more investigating to do.

Besides, I wasn't a fool. I brought home the bacon, but Malcolm was truly the breadwinner. He provided the eggs, toast, and orange juice to complete the meal. I'd have been a fool to let that go without a fight. I made sure that all those chicks got were time because I swiped that platinum card often, and for the most expensive shit. In the meantime I stacked my checks and about 30 percent of his every two weeks to build a cushion. My girls were accustomed to a certain lifestyle and they were going to have that if I could help it.

14

Glen Burnie, Maryland

When I pulled up on Mayo Road about two hours after leaving Philly I took in the sites. This was a nice suburban neighborhood. Quiet. Like they had an active neighborhood watch, and nosey neighbors. It didn't make me a bit of difference. What I had to do would be quick. As I slow rolled through the neighborhood I noticed that it was trash day from all the cans lined up on the curbs. This must have been my lucky day because I definitely had some trash to drop off here.

It didn't take me long to find the house I was looking for, and from the Benz parked outside I could only assume that he was taking care of her as well. Pulling from my purse a picture that I downloaded from the Internet, I stared at the woman who lived here. The one who was wrecking the flow in my household and part of the reason for my husband's demise. Not only were the fucking, but this bitch had a baby by my man. Unacceptable.

I wasn't going to blow up her spot though. I just had a little gift for her. See, if she thought for one second that having Malcolm's baby solidified her position she was sadly mistaken. I was his *only,* fuck being number one. And let me just say this for all the mistresses out there: a cheating man does not always mean that the one he has at home is not handling her business. I was a performer, you hear me? I invented seduction, and I made him feel like man. It became very obvious after a while that my loving husband had found someone else to keep him warm, but that was not because I couldn't; it was because I no longer wanted to. Wives don't need help, mistresses need to learn how to play their position. If you were supposed to have the number one spot you would already be in it. Understand?

Malcolm didn't want for anything. He came home to a clean, neat house, dinner every night, breakfast every morning, and he could fuck me in all three holes as often as he wanted. A period didn't stop a damn thing in my house. That was just a matter of a quick douche and a towel on the bed, and it was on and popping. I swallowed that crooked-dick nigga down to the base without gagging, and slurped up every drop. There wasn't a bitch alive who could touch me. So for the record, Malcolm got what he needed. Trust me. He was just a greedy bastard who didn't know my worth.

I will admit that I was the most hurt to find out about her though. Sherri Johnson . . . that was her name. She took away from my family when she had a child of her own. At least now I know why he was spazzing so hard when I got pregnant the second time around. He already had two mouths to feed.

How I found out about her was so retarded that I wanted to off Malcolm's ass sooner. That's the problem with guys. They don't know how to cheat and keep shit regular at home. At any rate, Malcolm traveled in and out of the city a lot for his job, but that wasn't my issue with him. He was spending an awful lot of time in Maryland, and it wasn't because they had good crab cakes.

Being the wife that I was, of course I checked in on my husband's whereabouts, how he spent his money, and where he was spending his time outside of work and away from his family. My husband was slick though, and knowing who you are dealing with is half the battle. Of course I booked him five-star hotel rooms while he was doing business, and, yes, he always checked out in enough time to get back home, but I was smart enough to know that he didn't always spend his nights at the hotel. Especially considering that on more than one occasion I called the hotel and he didn't answer.

What he wasn't banking on was the connections I had in Maryland. Being a television personality we got to meet all types of people, and when I lucked out and found out that a good friend of mine has a daughter who worked at the hotel that my husband always stayed at I set a plan into action. I needed all of my ducks to line up perfectly, so when I took the couple hundred dollars from my husband's account to pay her, she promptly sent me the four photos I asked for, all time stamped from the hotel security room: one of my husband checking in, one of him leaving the hotel without his bags an hour later, one of him coming back to the hotel hours later, and the last of him checking out.

I didn't say anything at the time because I knew that I would need more evidence than that. To make it easier, every time he went out of town I made sure to book his hotel so that I was certain he was staying in the same place. At first I was getting the same pictures of the same routine until one day little Miss Sherri popped into the picture. The kiss at the check-in desk and the embrace at the entrance the next morning was all I needed to see. This went on for a while, and that wasn't the only thing I noticed. From the last set of pictures that I got from my connect a few weeks ago, she had a belly that was growing. No doubt that it was Malcolm's fourth child. Too bad it would never get to meet its father.

That child saved her ass though, because I was actually on my way to Maryland to off her ass, too, and add to my bone collection, but my conscience wouldn't let me kill a pregnant woman so she got to live. Lucky her.

I pulled up and killed the engine, parking in the spot closest to the neighbor's house. I didn't know if they had police patrolling the area, or cameras up, but then I decided it didn't matter because I was going down for this shit anyway. Grabbing a pair of those thick yellow dish gloves I hopped out and walked around to the back, opening the door to the trunk of my truck. It started to smell a little funny back here, and I was hoping by the time I made it to North Carolina that I wouldn't die from the stench.

Taking a look at all the bags, I reached in and searched through until I found the bag that was labeled with her name on it. Each bag had a name for every mistress he slept with (or at least the ones I knew about), and I would be dropping off a body part to each ho who helped separate us since they helped separate him . . . literally. They would have to find his body as I spread him out across the states. Hell, he was spreading himself out anyway, so I figured I would give him that in death.

Once I found her bag, I pulled it out and drop it on top of the little pull cart that I purchased just for this. His limbs were too heavy to just carry around. I mean, I was just a woman. He was heavy as hell. Even though they were still heavy, it was easier to pull them than to carry.

Every light was out in her house and the surrounding houses so I hustled to make my move. Finally making it to the door, I opened up the bag to see what I had in hers. Everything was really covered in blood, and it smelled horrible, but I had already committed to this so the job had to be done. Just inside her screen door I placed Malcolm's mangled penis and testicles, his tongue, and both of his hands. These were the body parts that he used to please her and create two kids with her so she could have them. He wouldn't need them, after all.

Once the bag was empty of the parts I tilted the bag up to let the blood that had collected at the bottom drain out in the doorway and all down the steps. She could clean up the mess if she could stomach it herself. Folding the bag up, I tucked it neatly inside of a tote bin that I had in the back of the truck. My job here was done. I had a few more stops to make, and I needed to get there within the next few days if I could help it.

I got back inside my truck and started it up. As bad as I wanted to smash her fuckin' face in, it wasn't all her fault. I was sure Malcolm was feeding her some bullshit that brought her right in, and once she got to feel that good dick down she couldn't let go if she wanted to. He had that voodoo dick, and after that first shot you were stuck for life.

Shaking my head, I made a lazy U-turn and headed back toward I-95 heading to Prince George's County. I had a bone to pick with someone there as well. I hated that it even had to come to this, but when a good wife has gone bad, she's gone forever.

I checked to make sure that all ten of the pills I counted out were still there. I would need those by the time I got to where I needed to be. Now, you're probably thinking I'm a monster right? That's an easy conclusion to come to since you are on the outside looking in, but just about every woman in the world has taken a walk in my shoes. I'm just the only one brave enough to take things into my own hands. Well, I can't say that. I've watched enough episodes of *Snapped* to know that bitches do crazy shit all the time.

I thought my shit out a little more though, and at least had the courtesy to set shit up for my kids before I set my plan into action. No, it wasn't fair to them or my family, but I couldn't see living life without Malcolm so he had to go. At least that way I knew where he was and I didn't have to play the game of pretending like he wasn't fucking around when I knew he was. It was just too exhausting to live that way. What's done is done. Don't judge me. Or judge me if you want. It doesn't matter to me either way. But since you all in my business, you might as well let me vent, so get ready for the ride.

15

Being Mrs. Malcolm Bernard

Being the wife of Malcolm Bernard came with its fair share of benefits, and a level of stress that was sometimes too overwhelming to deal with. A regular bitch would never be able to rock with him the way I did. Like I said, he was a power player who was high on the chain of command. He wasn't sitting in the CEO chair, but next in line was better than not. Malcolm made shit happen, and every move he made was strategic. It had to be, in the production industry. You could be a hot commodity one minute, and the very next a has-been. With that being said he stayed in command and demand because if nothing else, people knew that Malcolm Bernard was a miracle worker. He could make sugar out of shit, and all that jazz.

The company he worked for had a few studios spread out south of Philadelphia, and Malcolm often visited these studios to make sure that the various projects he had going were running the way they should and in a timely manner. I had no complaints about Malcolm being gone from home so much in the beginning. Hell, it was part of the business, and what made it possible to afford the lavish lifestyle we lived. I also was not delusional about the freaks in the business. Malcolm exuded power and money, and naturally desperate hoes flocked to him in hopes of knocking me from my spot and sitting at number one. I couldn't blame them really because he made it easy for women to flirt. He was an attention whore, and loved that every eye was always on him. It's just that sometimes he allowed his dick to do the talking for him, and he couldn't always handle the outcome of a slaying. The problem came in for me when his extracurricular activities started to affect the home front.

Malcolm created magic on the set. He could turn a beast into a beauty queen, and drop the hottest beat on a cut that would have the entire club dropping it low and sweeping the floor. It was like he had the Midas touch, but everything he touched turned to platinum. It was like flashing lights followed him, and the whole world moved to the beat of the drums in his head. He had his hand in everything from the writing of the script to the soundtrack and everything in between. He was the man, plain and simple.

We looked good as a couple . . . a unit. My curvaceous size twelve, even after two kids, fit snuggly at his side. I had a flawless face, skin the color of coffee with a dab of cream, and the perfect attributes. My video-girl booty and breasts that looked perfect in a Vicky's bra kept heads turning. My long black hair flowed on some Beyoncé-type shit, and I kept it laid because as the wife of Malcolm Bernard you had to always be on point. We stayed red carpet ready. Being on the news every morning was a job in itself as well, and I was no doubt the prettiest weather girl on the East Coast.

At some point though, all of the finagling had to come to an end. Like I said, when he stopped coming home at night I started formulating my plan to get his ass back. Not back to me, but back for good. Nobody was going to have him. I won't lie and say that once the damage was done I did think that maybe I had taken it too far, but at that point I had no choice but to move forward. Since I was going to go down in history for it anyway I might as well make it a story worth telling. You know . . . go out with a *bang!*

I was a pure actress when I put my vacation time in, telling my boss that I was surprising my husband with a much-needed trip out of the States. They didn't know I would spread his trifling ass across the States, but it was none of their business. Either way I covered my tracks; that way when shit hit the fan they wouldn't be looking for me to show up at work as they would already be under the impression that I had taken the week off. It was better that way. No one was going to believe that the hottest weather girl and producer of an equally hot morning show, *Te'Nae at Ten,* was behind such a gruesome murder. By the time they caught on I would already be where I needed to be and my plan would be executed.

So, as I said, being Mrs. Bernard came with benefits. Chauffeured rides, diamond facials, Tiffany jewels, and Louis Vuitton everything. I didn't really have to work, but I was never one to sit back and not pull my share so I put my master's degree to good use. What I didn't bank on was the blatant disrespect. I never really got used to the late-night calls, and when I did show up on the set, from the ugly looks I got from the chicks there I could always tell which ones had already gotten dicked down and which ones were next in line. They acted like I was in the way. I mean, he was my husband. *Mine.* Maybe they didn't get that part. Sucking his dick in his trailer before a shoot could only do one thing and that was getting you more camera time. Regardless of how many times you swallowed his nut I had my hand where it counted: in his bank account.

That didn't mean I didn't have feelings. Malcolm was supposed to love only me. I know he didn't love those video chicks, but what did they have that I didn't? Wasn't

I enough? All of this shit was tearing me up on the inside and just added to the list of reasons why he had to die.

I almost swerved and lost control when my song came across the airwaves of 96.3 WHUR. This song described Malcolm and me to the letter, and every time I heard it made me fall deeper in love with him. Reaching forward, I turned the volume up a little more and sang from my soul as tears ran down my face.

""'Cause we made it this far on for better or worse. I wanna feel it even if it hurts. If I gotta cry to get to the other side, let's go 'cause we're gon' survive oh.'" I sang along with the lyrics. You couldn't tell me I wasn't Tamar Braxton on stage. The lyrics spoke to me, and it was cleansing to a certain extent.

We had good times. At one point we were inseparable. The pictures around my house proved that. I mentally went through the photos of our wedding day as I drove down this dark road. It was getting closer to morning, and I was hoping to make it to PG County before the sun came up completely and people starting stirring. I would have to spend the day here, but I had my hotel set up under an alias in the area so I wasn't concerned. Besides, it was about time to come up out of this diaper. I did believe I had gone enough in it.

When I pulled into the extended-stay parking lot, I parked in the back away from the other cars so that if anyone had indeed seen me leaving the cul-de-sac I didn't want them to readily point out my vehicle. That and a weird smell was starting to make itself known in my truck, no doubt from the decomposing body in the back. I put my hair up in a ponytail and made sure that my hat covered most of my face as I checked in and made it to my room unscathed. I didn't want to get caught before it was time because then all of this would have been for nothing.

Although the room was nice it offered little comfort for me. I was still trying to wrap my mind around what I had done. I was convinced that I shouldn't feel bad about it. After all, he called this on himself. All he had to do was be a loving and devoted husband, and show me the same respect I showed him. He wasn't the only hot commodity on the scene. I got offers all the time, but I never took anyone up on it, ever. I flashed this heavy diamond on my hand every time someone approached me because I was happy at home. I was Mrs. Malcolm Bernard. I got all the perks. I had the kids, the house, and the ring. Come to find out, all of that didn't mean a damn thing at the end of the day.

I popped one of the Vicodin and chased it with a swig of Hennessy, hoping it would make it work faster. Afterward I chewed on a piece of toast that I snagged from the free breakfast the hotel offered so that I wouldn't get sick. I knew that this was going to get wild the longer I traveled, but I was prepared for the ride. At the end of the day I refused to live with regrets. *The only regret I will have is that my children won't have their parents.* They were probably better off without us anyway, or at least that was the logic I used to comfort my restless spirit as I drifted off to sleep.

16

PG County

I never understood why they built DC to have just one road in and one road out. What kind of shit is that? I mean, everywhere you went always led back to this one dumb-ass road. As I made my way up to Prince George's County, the red numbers on the clock in my car read 1:23 a.m. The pills did exactly what I needed them to do, and I didn't wake up again until almost midnight. I was starving when I woke up, but it was something that would have to be handled later.

Once I left PG County I was headed out to Virginia, and I needed to make good time on the road. After relieving myself, I stepped into another adult diaper, making sure that everything was secure before putting on my sweats and my boots. I made sure that I had all of my belongings, and I wiped everything down in the hotel room that I had touched so that my fingerprints wouldn't be readily available. I saw that on an episode of *Criminal Minds* once. Who knew it would come in handy?

As I drove I reflected on the good times Malcolm and I had and how it was so sad that he had to go. I remembered our wedding day, and I was so nervous about getting married. Just the week before we had gotten into horrible argument about some bitch I had found out about, and it was one of those moments where you knew you had a chance to get out but you didn't. After all, I was carrying his baby, and I was not beat to be going through the child support/custody battle. I knew Malcolm would offer me a life that I would achieve a lot faster with him than without. Red flags waving, I showed up at the justice of the peace, ready to sign on the dotted line. I told him on that day, "You fuck with me, you stuck with me." Maybe he thought I was joking.

At any rate, I had a list that I was following. I knew where I had to be and how fast I had to be there in order to not be caught by the police before I got to my final destination. I didn't know that pulling off this kind of shit took so much work. I used to always say that I would never allow someone to have me open like this, but Malcolm definitely had me at the top of the crazy list.

It was weird how everything fell into place. Malcolm came home from yet another road trip late as hell and smelling like some cheap-ass perfume. Lately it was getting to the point where he didn't even try to hide the fact that there were other chicks involved. Lipstick on the collar of his shirts and boxers was evidence that he was out doing no good. One time he had come in and I saw a least three different colors of lipstick on his boxers when I went to do the wash, and it made me wonder if this fool had gone to a rainbow party. I knew when it came time for him to hang out in the studio that oftentimes it got wild in there, but at least he could try to spare my feelings a little.

He came home that night like it was a regular night. I made sure that I had a spectacular meal made for us and everything. His bathwater was ready, and even though I smelled the sex coming off of his skin, I acted like everything was Kool & the Gang as I laid out his bathrobe while he bathed. I was beyond pissed at him. How could he so freely throw everything away that we had? It wasn't just about me, we had kids. It felt like none of that even mattered to him, and now his life didn't matter to me. By the time he got to the dining room his plate was piping hot and waiting for him along with a chilled glass of wine.

He looked appreciative as he made his way to the dining area in his robe and slippers, looking like the man of the house. Both plates were set by candlelight, and I had on a robe as well. I had on a lingerie-type top so that it would appear like he was going to get the best ride of his life, but I already had my clothes in the basement along with everything that I would need to get the job done.

He sat down to his food, and I joined him. His drink was laced with a double dose of Prolixin . . . an odorless, tasteless drug used to treat schizophrenic patients. When used correctly it helps with hallucinations and things associated with the disorder, but with the lethal dose that I gave him he would surely be dead before he could even finish his plate. This drug could be detected in his bloodstream, but it dissipated so fast it would look like he died from natural causes. That didn't matter though, because by the time I got done with him he wouldn't have a bloodstream to search through.

I enjoyed my meal as he took hearty helpings of his, downing his glass of wine in two big gulps. I didn't bother to engage him in any conversation. I just went ahead and let him do him. It started getting real interesting as his head began to loll around on his neck like he was drunk. His mouth went slack, and a long line of drool hung from his mouth. I didn't blink as his body suddenly became rigid and he fell to the side, hitting his head hard on the floor. I continued my meal as his labored breaths turned into slow, shallow breaths as he lay on the floor, and then eventually nothing came from him at all.

I thought I would be grossed out by his reaction to the

medicine, but it didn't bother me not one bit. It actually happened way quicker than I expected and I was kind of relieved that it was finally over. Now I wouldn't have to worry about his late-night bullshit with women who only wanted his money. I wasn't fazed by this at all, surprisingly, and I thought I would feel some type of regret. I even stepped over his body as I helped myself to a second plate while he breathed his last breath. Afterward I smoked a cigarette and kicked my feet up on the table. By now he'd been dead for a while, but I wanted to give the medicine a chance to really work. What I was about to do was unforgivable, and I needed to have my head on straight to get this done.

I got up and kicked the shit out of him a few good times before going to put my sweats on for phase two of the plan. I was happy that my sister decided to keep the kids for me. I convinced her that I wanted a romantic evening with my husband before we left, and I included a card that I told her not to open up until the morning. She got the same story as everyone at my job. We were going on vacation. That way, when it came time for questioning she wouldn't have to be involved.

Once the dishes and everything was cleared away I put on my sweats and boots and commenced dragging his heavy body to the basement. Dead weight was serious, and I actually had to stop a few times even before getting him to the basement doorway. Once there I positioned his body at the edge of the steps and let him free fall the rest of the way down to the bottom. He was dead so it ain't like he felt any of it. At the bottom I dragged him over to the black tarp that I purchased from Home Depot with the same gift card that I used to pay for the hotel room and pretty much fund this entire adventure. I didn't want to use either my card or Malcolm's for two reasons. Reason one: I didn't want them to be able to trace it back to me. Reason two: I didn't want them to freeze my account in any way. My sister would need to access that money to take care of our kids.

It took me longer than I thought, but I finally got his body on to the tarp, naked and spread out. The bath thing was genius! He really didn't have a lot of clothes on, so stripping him wasn't an issue at all. As I stood above him, staring at his naked body, I got a twitch in my pussy as thoughts of him moving inside, on top, and around me flashed through my mind. If nothing else, Malcolm had some good dick.

Once I secured a plastic apron, gloves, and a clear face mask over my body I looked at him to decide where to start. Grabbing an extra sharp Wusthof and Henckels butcher knife, I wondered if Malcolm was regretting in his death ever buying me those expensive-ass knives in the first place. I walked around him, trying to decide where to start. Rigor mortis had already started to set in some, and from what I found out on Google, at the three-hour point he might be completely stiff, and it would make it harder to cut through his flesh.

His dick was standing at attention, as I circled him, looking like a yummy chocolate pole. I resisted the urge to take him for a ride one last time, and decided that his dick would be the first thing to go. Kneeling down before him I did indulge in a deep throat one last time before grabbing the shaft and cutting him at the base. The taste of his dick in my mouth would be something for me to take on the road. After removing his dick, and going back for the testicles, I was in the zone. I had six bags labeled and ready for the parts because that would be the only way to get him to the car.

Now, I already dropped the contents of the first bag off, and was on my way to deliver bag number two.

"Earlier today, a gruesome discovery of male genitalia

was found on a doorstep covered in blood right in our Glen Burnie, Maryland area. Sources are not saying who the body parts belong to, but the investigation has started. They appeared there as the homeowner came out of the house for work, slipping on the blood and falling down the steps. Sources say she was seven months pregnant, and may have lost her baby. More to come after this commercial break. . . ."

The radio personality interrupted my thoughts with this news. As of right now they didn't know who was behind it, and there wasn't anything said about someone seeing my truck parked near there. I stepped on the gas a little harder so that I could get to my second destination faster. I could not get caught before it was over. I had to make it to the end. That would be the only peace of mind I would have in death.

17

Mistress Number Two

I arrived in Prince George's County, and was in love with the neighborhood. I could clearly see myself residing in the gated communities. The expensive cars and pristine surroundings were beautiful and serene at this time of the morning. The people around here clearly had money, and it made me look at Malcolm a little differently. At least he messed with women who were about something. I had yet to pull up in a raggedy neighborhood.

I quickly found Tulip Grove Drive, and although it wasn't gated, it was a pretty nice neighborhood with single homes that sat way back from the curb. Checking the address, I found the house that I was looking for and came to a slow crawl. Scouting the area, I looked for the same things that I looked for at the previous stop. I saw no signs of cameras or people out walking dogs so I made my move quickly. Leaving my car running and leaving the door partially open I rounded the back to search through the bags. This one was more personal because I had seen this woman on a few of his sets. She worked as his assistant, and I could see she had the hots for him.

I remembered her clearly because she was one of the few who gave me stank looks and a bad attitude whenever I was around, like I had no business being around my husband. Malcolm actually had to check her ass one time because she was acting very unprofessional toward me, but he never fired her like I requested. Probably because she did shit to him that I wouldn't dare. I was one of the biggest freaks in the city of Philadelphia, but apparently these Maryland girls had us beat.

After I found out about the first chick, I hired a private investigator to see what else my dear husband was up to. I was certain there had to be more than one, but it didn't soften the blow or lessen the shock when I found out about the others. It was weird because all of us favored a little. Complexion, long hair, curves, and kids. I guessed it was better to deal with someone with obligations; that way they couldn't be bothered with you all the time. He was a smart man, and wouldn't deal with anyone who had too much time on their hands. You had to be about something to be with Malcolm, although I was sure some may have slipped through the cracks.

This one was a bitch though. The most possessive of them all. She fawned over Malcolm, and when she was around none of his other assistants could do anything right in her eyes. She stayed ten steps ahead of everyone, and knew what Malcolm needed before he even knew he needed it. She was dangerous and definite competition. I was sure that she was giving him what he needed and more, and once the pictures showed up with them having sex outdoors and in all kinds of positions it confirmed everything. Yeah, she gave him the ass, and that's how she won him over. I called her the dragon lady because she was a fire-breathing bitch who caused havoc for everyone around her. It was like she had Malcolm trapped in a castle like a male Rapunzel, and she was stalking the castle, keeping anyone away who could rescue him. The bitch had to go, and I was the right one to do it.

Imagine how ecstatic I was when I found out that Malcolm had a key to the house he helped her buy. Found that tidbit of info out by looking through his financial records. The deed was in his name only, but she was on the mortgage. She had a son, but it was from a previous relationship, and he lived with his father throughout the school year and stayed the summers with her. This was perfect because that meant he wouldn't be home and I wouldn't have to off him, too. I didn't plan on leaving any witnesses. If she had a goldfish up in there consider it flushed. Just like with Sherri, I wasn't going to kill this girl at first either, but she was such a bitch I felt like the world could do without her. Sherri only got spared because she was pregnant; this one didn't have the same pass to save her ass.

Taking the key from my pocketbook after setting down the trash bags containing the body parts that would be left here, I piled everything up at the back door. I parked my car a little farther down so that if things went wrong the evidence wouldn't be right in front of the door. Letting myself in, I punched in the code that I found in his books and I was surprised that it worked. She gave him more power than I thought. I had a silencer on my gun because I didn't need to have gunshots going off in this quiet-ass neighborhood.

She was stupid. I had been texting her with Malcolm's phone throughout the night just to see where her head was at. She loved him. After reading through his text messages and seeing the type of conversation they had I already knew what I needed to do to get her involved. She thought Malcolm was showing up there at around nine in the morning, and she was instructed to get her sleep because they would be spending the day together in bed. She was so gullible, and when I typed in the three words that every side chick wanted to hear she melted like better. Saying "I love you" always pushed a bitch off her square and I had her with her guard down the way I needed her.

"You know the code, right?" she texted his phone. Of course I asked her to confirm it to be sure.

"3-4-7-7?" I texted back the wrong number to get her reply.

"No silly. It's your birthday, remember. Just type in 0-5-1-8."

"Okay. I love you," I responded.

"I love you more."

I wanted to throw up. I wasn't concerned though because today was her last day around. Once I walked in and punched in the code, I looked around the house to see what was going on. It was cute. You could tell they dropped a few dollars decorating, but it wasn't anywhere near as lavish or clean as my house. A slim layer of dust covered everything, and I made me wish that I could do a quick run through and wet dust the place. *All I do to keep my space spotless, and this fool liked being around dust mites.* A damn shame.

Creeping up the steps, I checked to see if there was anyone else in the house. I knew her son wasn't there, but she could have had him there and was going to get rid of him in the morning before Malcolm showed up. Satisfied that we were alone I walked down the hall to the last bedroom door. Taking a deep breath I tested the knob. Surprisingly I wasn't nervous. I had gone through this scenario in my head a million times already, and I could only hope that it would play out the same way.

When I opened the bedroom door I could see her sleeping silhouette lying in the middle of the bed. I started to plug one in her right from the doorway, but I wanted her to see my face before she died so that she knew I did it. I would just meet her in hell afterward. She was a sound sleeper because there was no way possible someone would be able to move freely through my house like this without me knowing it.

I clicked on the lamp on the nightstand and tapped her softly with the butt of the gun to wake her. She stretched and moaned a little before opening her eyes. She seemed happy that "Malcolm" had shown up early, but the smile fell right from her face when she saw me standing there.

"Hey, Lexi. Long time no see."

"What the fuck are you doing in my house? Where is Malcolm?" she questioned, both surprised and livid.

"He's downstairs," I replied nonchalantly. "I heard you liked wrapping your legs around him while y'all fucked so I brought you a gift."

"Bitch, are you—"

A shot to the head silenced her before she could complete her sentence. A neat little hole rested on the side of her head as she lay with her eyes open staring at the ceiling. Placing the gun in my bag, I went downstairs and brought both the bags I brought in with me upstairs. Placing my gloves on, I reached in the bloody bag that smelled like rotting flesh and positioned both of his legs and his torso between hers, positioning her legs around his headless body. Since she liked him on top of her that's how she would have him. Tilting the bag, I poured out all of the fluid that had collected at the bottom on the top of both of them, folding the bag afterward so that I could take it out with me. Grabbing a towel I wiped my prints from all the knobs I had touched, and as I left I set the code to secure the house.

This location I wasn't really concerned about right now because it would be a few days before they found her body. I even wiped off Malcolm's phone and left it there just in case they wanted to track it via GPS. That way it wouldn't be with me later on when they caught up with me.

Getting back into my truck I noticed one of her neighbors had come out to walk his dog, and I wondered why he was out this time of morning, but whatever. I tucked my head down farther so that he couldn't get a clear view of me, and before he could say a word I was in my truck, pulling off. I didn't draw any attention to myself by pulling off all quickly and looking suspicious; I just rolled out like I was in no rush to get any particular place. I was coming down the block on the pavement so he didn't see where I had come from, so I was cool. Back on the road I was headed to where I needed to be. From what was being talked about on the radio, the police still had no clue who the body parts belonged to, and who had left them there. Things were going better than planned, and it made me smile to know I was finally getting things to go my way.

18

Captain Save a Ho

You may be wondering what brings a person to get to the point where I was now. Was I jealous? Or maybe even possessive? Why didn't I just leave Malcolm and start all over, right? Did I suffer from low self-esteem? The answer is simple. He belonged to me. I put in years and earned my title and the right to be respected as Malcolm's wife. The children were an investment and we were supposed to be happy. Not going through this type of bullshit that we had going on right now.

There was a time in our life where I was really doing me. I had a steady rotation—a stable, if you will—of able-bodied men who would do anything to serve me. Not that I was addicted to sex, but I wanted what I wanted when I wanted it, and if one wasn't available I always backed up the backup. Malcolm and I were in a sort of in-between stage where he was out doing him as well, and just as I was a part of his rotation he was a part of mine. Everything was good though, because we had yet to talk about getting serious. Things were starting to take off in both of our careers, and neither of us were ready to settle down because we were too busy enjoying the limelight.

We were happy for the most part. I mean, I was really enjoying life. I had just gotten the green light for my news program, *Te'Nae at Ten,* which gave me the stage to discuss the things I loved. Fashion! Every woman wanted to be beautiful, and I got an hour every day after the morning news to discuss makeup tips, shoes, and clothes.

My favorite segment was "Style on a Budget," where I showed women how to look like the stars but with less money. I was ecstatic the producers even okayed it, and once the ratings came in after the first season, the show had been a mainstay and was one of the most watched morning shows.

The show really took off once I started having special guests on my show, and once talks of a real set came into play I knew I had made it big time. I was a weather girl at heart, so although I had gained a control for my show, I was still allowed to do the weather for my beloved city of Philadelphia. I was living my dream, and I was happy.

On the flip side, Malcolm was making a name for himself as well. He was producing more and more behind the music scene, and when he decided to dabble in the film industry it was the best decision he ever made. He was genius with a script, and his background in the music business came in handy when it came time to lay music for a soundtrack. Malcolm could make any vision come to life, and he was good at it. Hell, he was the best at it, and that's how he climbed the popularity ladder so quickly.

We all know that with fame comes power, and with power comes arrogance. Malcolm knew he was the man, and sometimes it went to his head. At one point no one was able to tell him any damn thing. This man thought his shit didn't stink like the rest of ours, and it was more of a headache to deal with him than anything. He had bitches flocking and running at his very command, and I had to admit that when we first ran across each other I was not checking for him like that. I actually couldn't stand his ass, and trust and believe he had to work for this shit.

It had been awhile since Malcolm and I had a romp in the hay because we were busy being single, and building our careers. I ran into a guy on my set who did makeup for Malcolm on the sets of a few music videos that he had produced, and he was telling me how much of a monster he was and how difficult it could be to work for him. Malcolm was a perfectionist, which came off as very annoying to everyone around him. I almost couldn't believe the things he was telling me as he did my makeup for my new segment, but I knew Malcolm well enough for it to have some truth to it so I decided that I needed to reach out to Malcolm to maybe reel him in some. I didn't think it would turn into a relationship and later marriage, but hindsight is twenty-twenty, and if we knew everything up front there would be no room for experience and growth. At any rate, I decided that I would hit Malcolm up later in the day to see what was going on, and maybe see how I could help him if needed.

After my segment I sent Malcolm a text, just saying hey, and surprisingly he hit me right back.

I miss you, girl! How you been? *the text read. I was shocked a little because Malcolm wasn't the "I miss you" type, but people change all the time so I just rolled with it.*

I'm living *I responded with a smile on my face. Thoughts of him in the bed reminded me that it had been awhile since I'd been worked out by anyone. When you are building a brand, it's so hard to fit in personal time, and it clicked at that moment that Malcolm might have been having the same issue. That was probably why he was being so damn mean to everyone.*

Yeah, I see you big time so you don't have time for little old me *he responded with a smiley face behind it. He always could make me smile.*

Not as big as you, boo *I respond and then quickly added,* So are you in the city tonight?

No, but I can be. Should I be?

Do you think you should?

I'll see you in a few hours.

I didn't even bother to respond. It had been awhile since we'd connected like that and I knew it would be worth the wait. He was probably in Maryland, which was only about two to two and a half hours away from

Philly, depending on where in Maryland he was, and if he was leaving right away. That gave me time to go home and get everything in order.

Now, around this time he had his own place and I had mine. We had yet to move into the place we had, but I always kept immaculate surroundings so I wasn't worried about the appearance of my place at all.

I knew how Malcolm liked his women, so I went to work making sure that any unnecessary hair was removed. Malcolm liked his garden completely naked, and I loved the slippery feeling I got from it so had my driver stop at the European Wax Spa on the way to my house so that I could get right. I was elated that the woman I usually saw was there and could fit me in, so once I was snatched bald I skipped a few blocks down to Vicky's so that I could put on something he had yet to see so that he could clearly see what he had been missing.

I got home a little after noon, and I still had time to take a long bath in rose-scented water. It left a nice heady aroma that was light and sensual, and worked well with my pheromones. I made sure that my body was nice and moist, not too greasy, and my hair was still looking studio fresh as I slipped into a crotchless thong and matching teddy. Right on schedule, I received a text that he had just touched down at the Philadelphia International Airport, so he must have already been en route here because that was too fast to have been in the office and had to have booked a flight. I quickly put together a fondue tray of a few fresh strawberries, pineapple chunks, red grapes, and a few dipping sauces. I wasn't sure if we were even going to be able to get to the food, but I wanted to have it there just in case shit got wild.

Within forty-five minutes I was stretched across my bed waiting for Malcolm to get here. We had exchanged keys years ago, and only used them when we knew we were going to be in each other's company. There was never an instance when we would pop up unexpected.

*That wasn't the nature of our relationship. We weren't
a couple; we simply indulged in each other until we had
enough. Sometimes more . . . that's how we did things.
We never crossed each other's space without permission,
and I thought that's why it worked out for us for so long.
We weren't married; we simply enjoyed each other's
company, so there were no hard feelings about anyone
else. There was a mutual respect, and we didn't flaunt
those we were dealing with in each other's face.*

Things changed once I got pregnant and we got married. I'm not saying that having my baby was a mistake,
but I think going in we both knew that it kind of was.
Either way, that day it was all about achieving the ultimate orgasm, and we were both ready to make it happen.

*What I liked about Malcolm is he wasn't a selfish
lover. His goal was to always make sure you had more
than you can handle. I more than liked it. I loved that
about him. That made me want to give him more also. I
knew it was going to be electric, and I was pulsating all
over in anticipation. I unarmed the house and made sure
the covers were tucked tight before I positioned myself
seductively in the bed. I couldn't wait to feel him inside
of me, and I was already starting to get wet just thinking
about it.*

*When I heard the door open and close my heart started
beating a little faster. I was like a kid in the window of a
chocolate factory and I couldn't wait to get in and taste
all the treats. I sat up by the headboard with my feet
tucked under me, and all of my hair flowed to one side
over my shoulder the way he liked it in big curls. My
lip gloss was minimal but popping nonetheless because
pretty soon it would be coating the base of his dick, and
I couldn't wait to taste it.*

*He looked pleasantly surprised when he finally saw
me . . . like he was looking at a long-lost friend. I didn't*

say a word; I just allowed him the time to take it all in. The Pink Sands Yankee Candle I had burning had the room smelling delectable, and the sheer pink of my lingerie matched up perfectly. My breasts sat at attention, and my chocolate skin had a soft glow the emanated in the dim light of the room. I had the blinds and curtains drawn to block out the afternoon sun so that I could appear later in the day, and I was ready for him.

He looked at me with a want in his eyes that I had never seen before, and it made me realize how long it had truly been since we were together like this. He took his time and undressed just like I liked it, first kicking off no doubt an expensive pair of Italian leather shoes that he neatly set near the ottoman at the end of my bed. It was almost like he was putting on a show as he slipped out of a cute corduroy jacket and draped it just as neatly over the chair in the corner of the room. I was practically salivating as the buttons came undone by his agile fingers, and I couldn't wait for them to strum across my body in that same fashion.

All he had left was his wife beater, jeans, and boxers, and I loved how he looked almost thug. His wife beater looked extra white against his milk chocolate skin, and I wanted him to melt all over me. When he unbuttoned his pants they rested on his hips, and his muscles rippled as he pulled his shirt up and over his head. I wanted to jump off the bed and wrap around him like a cobra, but I kept my cool. This was the ritual. It's how we did things, and good things came to those who waited. He taught me that.

Once he was completely naked he strolled over to me and stood at the side of the bed, his flag at full staff ready to be saluted. Malcolm was thick and heavy, and that curve did something to my spirit that I couldn't explain. He had nice thick veins that run up the underside of it, and a smooth mushroom-shaped head that felt wonderful on my tongue. He had what I called that superhero dick, and everyone who got it was weakened like it was made of kryptonite. I loved it . . . more than I loved him.

I crawled over to the edge of the bed, pussy aching and dying to be fucked good, but I knew I had to taste him first. It was only right. Was I worried about diseases? Nope. We vowed that we would always use protection with others so that we wouldn't have to use it ourselves, and he never gave me reason to believe he wasn't following the rules. I gobbled him up immediately, taking it as close to the base as I could, while keeping his balls warm in my small palms. I slurped and spit all over that thing, and his moans just turned me on even more.

It took damn near both hands to hold him, and it wasn't until his knees were threatening to buckle that I let him loose and allowed him to get in the bed. He stretched out the full length of the bed, and I wasted no time getting on him. The minute we made contact, and his head found my slip, the water works began. I worked to the tip to lube it up with my natural juices before sucking him in, and clinching his length until he was in me fully. My walls expanded to allow him in my space then tightened back up like a vice grip. I didn't realize how much I missed him until then.

He moaned as he pushed both nipples together and sucked and slurped on them like milk might possibly come out. My body was on fire, and I felt like I was going crazy. I took my time riding him and savoring the moment. I wanted him to feel me wrapped all around him. It felt like the room was getting hotter as my orgasm approached, and my moans got louder and louder as my body began to crash.

"You gonna bust on daddy's dick?" His deep baritone voice bounced around in my head like a ping-pong *machine knocking me way out into the stratosphere. He grabbed my hips and pushed me down on him, meeting up with a hard thrust that sent me flying over the edge.*

I couldn't talk, I couldn't see, and I promise you I was on the verge of a blackout as he drilled into my Milky Way. I felt like I was drowning and fighting for dear life. He pushed me down on him and pulled me all the way up until he was completely out of me. My pussy felt extra hot like somebody lit a match to it, and a scream was building up in me that I almost couldn't contain. He flipped me over and laid me down on my back, and the moment his pillow soft lips made contact with my clit I squirted in release, coating his chin, neck and upper chest. It felt like a river flowed out of me, and I thought for sure my heart was going to stop. He didn't release his hold until my body subsided and I was kind of able to breathe again. That's how he got my ass that night. After wiping away my wetness with a towel he prepared me for round two. Shit, I was ready to go to sleep, but he had other plans for me.

"Oh no, pretty," he spoke into my ear as he slid into me from the side. "I'm not done with you."

We were on a spoon position, and he was slow stroking me. I bounced my ass on him and clinched down on him until he had me in a death grip and damn near singing in falsetto. He got me right back there with him, and we were able to explode at the same time. He didn't bother to pull out, which was surprising, but I had just gotten my period so I wasn't all the way worried about getting pregnant. At the time I was just enjoying the moment.

Malcolm was the man . . . real shit. And any chick who had him was stuck forever.

19

And Baby Makes Three

"Malcolm, I'm pregnant."

Silence . . . Like dead-ass silence on the other end of the phone. Malcolm and I had begun kicking it on the regular ever since that night he came to town. We weren't "dating" per se, but he was definitely wearing this pussy all the way out every chance he got. It was how we did things, and each time was a new and exciting adventure. We did things to each other that would surely send us both to hell in gasoline drawers, and we loved it. We never really thought about the lack of protection and honestly, I forgot about my birth control a long time ago. I guess I got comfortable. Too comfortable . . . and now I was sitting here with a stupid look on my pregnant face.

"How far are you?" he finally asked. I was sure he was just as shocked as I was by the news. We were having so much fun that I forgot all about my period. It wasn't until the dizzy spells started happening that I decided I needed to go to the doctor. I was barely making it through my segments, and even then being pregnant was the furthest thing from my mind. A little stomach bug had been going around the city for some time, and I figured I might have just been getting sick. Imagine the look on my face when the doctor asked me one simple question: when was my last period?

"I think it was like a month ago or maybe a little longer," I remembered telling the doctor. *I wasn't one of those people who marked that kind of stuff down so I couldn't give her an actual date even if I tried. It had been awhile though, and I realized that maybe I didn't have a stomach virus, but maybe there was something else in there causing havoc on my mornings.*

"No problem, let's just get some urine and a few tubes of blood to see what's going on. It's probably just a little bug. Something has definitely been going around lately." *I still didn't think anything of it as I filled a urine cup, and sat in the lab to get my blood drawn. I had so much on my plate with the show that I had been moving nonstop for days. Just about every night belonged to Malcolm, whether we Skyped a phone sex session or he was in the flesh giving me what I loved. I was really doing me and living my life. That was until . . .*

"Well, your urine tested positive for pregnancy. We will be preparing you for an ultrasound to see how far along you are, and the doctor will be in to talk to you soon after," the medical office assistant informed me as I sat reading a magazine in the patient room. I was floored and speechless. Pregnant? Me? Impossible! *Yet possible because she just told me I was. I was numb as I lay flat on the exam table with my shirt hiked up under my breasts. I didn't even flinch as she applied that ice-cold jelly to my belly, and began to move the little box thing around. It wasn't until she turned the sound up on the machine and the heartbeat echoed around the room that it all came into perspective. I was pregnant . . . by Malcolm. What the fuck would I do?*

"I'm fourteen weeks," I told him as I lay in the bed in a fetal in tears. I never wanted Malcolm to feel like I was trapping him. A baby was the last thing on my mind, but it happened. Now we had to figure out what we were going to do.

"It's okay. I'll be there in the morning so that we can figure it all out. Why are you crying?"

"I don't want you to think I trapped you, Malcolm. My career is just taking off, and so is yours. Are we ready for this?" I needed confirmation . . . I needed comfort. I needed him to understand that I was not like any of the women he may have been used to dealing with. It was not my intent to lock Malcolm down like this, and I wanted him to understand that.

"Daddy will take care of everything," he said in a soothing voice that instantly put me at ease. *"Wipe those tears from those pretty eyes. I'll be on the next thing smoking to Philly and we will figure it all out. Don't I always take care of you?"*

"Yes," I replied as I wiped snot and tears from my face and on my comforter.

"This will be no different. I'll see you in a few."

We both hung up without saying good-bye. My head was spinning with all kinds of thoughts, and I couldn't help but wonder where this would go and how things might change between us. What if he didn't want the baby? What if that messed up everything that he had going on? Could we really be exclusive? Most importantly, was I ready to be a mom? I lay back and stared at the ceiling for what felt like hours until I finally fell asleep.

I woke up a few hours later to Malcolm getting into bed with me, fully clothed. He pulled me into his chest and held me so tight. My tears flowed, soaking his shirt, and I felt even more confused than before.

"Baby girl, don't cry. Everything is going to be okay." He soothed me with his voice as he rubbed my back.

"You think so?"

"I know so. We got this," he confirmed as he leaned back to rub my belly. My stomach was still pretty flat to be so far along but the doctor said that I would start

showing soon.

His hands swirled around my belly in small circles, and eventually traveled up around my breasts, gently squeezing my tender nipples until a moan escaped my lips. He caught my moan in his mouth as he kissed me, and all of my stress melted away. We were having a baby, and he was okay with it. Everything after this was supposed to be a breeze. Hopefully the network would embrace my new belly, and we could even do a maternity segment on how to stay fashionable while pregnant. The ideas were flowing, and for the first time since I heard the news I actually felt like everything was really going to be okay.

We were lying still, listening to each other breathe, and I was sure thinking about the direction our life had turned. Malcolm suddenly got up from the bed, and grabbed his jacket from the chair. I sat up in the bed because I wasn't quite sure what was going on. He had the silliest look when he came back to the bed that I didn't really get so I sat mute, waiting for him to reveal the reason for his smile.

He sat back down on the bed, then knelt beside it, afterward placing a light blue box on top of the comforter. I just stared at it because I didn't want to assume there was something major inside of it. It could have very well have been a pair of diamond earrings, so I wasn't about to play myself. Malcolm bought me jewels and trinkets all the time.

"Go ahead and open it up."

Rocked up! Lucida cut with a diamond band . . . easily about two and a half carats . . . an engagement ring. I was speechless, and my entire body was shaking as I plucked it from the box and tried putting it on my finger. He actually had to slide it on my finger for me.

"I was planning to propose the next time I saw you.

I've had this ring for about three weeks now, so I don't want you to feel like you are getting this because you are pregnant. This was supposed to happen, and things are the way they are supposed to be."

I couldn't stop staring at my hand. It was gorgeous. I heard everything he said, but I couldn't respond. It was like I was in a movie, and I had met my Prince Charming.

"Te'Nae, will you marry me?"

"Yes, Malcolm, I'll marry you."

It was the happiest and most joyous moment of our lives I think. The best things come from unexpected moments, and I truly believed that. The worst things can come from an unexpected moment too, and unfortunately I learned both of those lessons from being with Malcolm. The same things that make you laugh will make you cry, and the same bitch you fuck over will make sure you die. The bad thing was he didn't see that coming . . . or did he?

20

What's Good for the Goose

I made it out of DC in what seemed like record time. For a split second, guilt started to set in about what I was doing, and what I had done. People cheat all the time. Did I really have to kill him? After thinking about it for half of a second more I decided that I did. I felt like Beyoncé in that "Ring the Alarm" song. Just like she said, "I'll be damned if I see another chick on your arm." Wasn't anyone going to have Malcolm if I couldn't have him, and I wasn't sharing the dick willingly. So I came to the conclusion that I had done the right thing. He had to go, and now he was gone.

I only had a few more bags in the trunk, and the stench was so bad I had to ride with the windows cracked. It was cold as hell outside, but I almost couldn't breathe with the odor in the truck so I decided to just ride with my coat on and the windows cracked. I didn't want to draw attention riding with the windows all the way down in frigid cold weather. That would surely have the police looking at me sideways. I really had no choice if I wanted to make it to my destination in time.

Turning on the radio, I was amused by the news on what was going on with me. Still there was no one who had a clue about what I had done. The radio announcer sounded like she was in such disbelief about what had happened. "Who would cut off someone's limbs and leave them on a doorstep?" She questioned the act as if it was the most horrible act in the world. Shit, many of women dreamed of doing what I did, but only a few of us are actually brave enough to pull it off. I wasn't crazy. Admitting that I was crazy would imply that I was mentally deranged, demented, or insane and that was furthest from the truth. There was nothing mental or deranged about me, and this was the most sane I'd ever been in my entire life. I was very aware of my actions, what I had done, and what I was about to do. I knew that I killed my husband because he cheated. I knew that I was dropping his body parts off to his mistresses and that I had killed one along the way, and I knew what I was going to do once I reached my final hotel room. I was actually quite organized and running on schedule. What crazy person you know can do all that? Yep, sane as the day is long, and there were no regrets.

As I was pulling up to my very last drop-off point I started to feel a sense of relief. After this it would be all over. I could do what I planned and not have to worry about anything. All of these women had a hand in fucking up my household. That's the part the mistress does not get. Rarely does a man leave his wife for the other woman. That shit doesn't even happen in movies anymore. When they say it's cheaper to keep her, truer words have never been spoken. Unless the wife agrees to separation or the man knows it will be drama free, then and only then will he go.

I also have to reiterate a point. Mistresses are under the impression that just because a man cheats the woman he has at home is doing something wrong. All of these simple bitches were sure that I was off my game. Partly because, I was sure, Malcolm made them believe I was. Men pillow talk and spill more milk than a child with chubby fingers. Always running they damn mouth trying to make these bitches feel secure. These day-after-the-holiday bitches.

These low-self-esteem, settle-for-anything, wishing-they-had-what-I-have bitches. I hate a mistress, a home wrecker, a side chick, a nut-ass wanna-be-me bitch. I felt like if you thought you could take my place and do a better job than me you were more than welcome to try, but know that you should come prepared to fill some big shoes. I was a boss, and I made shit happen. Know your position.

That wasn't even the thing that had me fired up the most. What had me on ten was the fact that all of these chicks knew me. It's not like no one knew Malcolm had a wife. It was a star-studded event. It was all over the TV and in the magazines. When Malcolm Bernard's single status switched to married the world knew. Our wedding photo was on the cover of *Essence* and *Jet* magazines, for God's sake. We were a power couple. People knew who we were.

But as I said, chicks always think that they can change someone. Men always give these birds super powers and they walk around thinking they're invincible. They tend to forget they are anything other than number one. This ain't no sharing-type situation. You are supposed to play the background and enjoy the benefits that came with being the side dip to a power house. The side chick always gets the goods. Diamonds, furs, trips . . . all that dumb shit that they thought I as the wife was missing out on, but already had in the bag. If they were smart they would just shut the fuck up, stroke his ego, stack they cash, and eat until the ride was over with enough to last them until they found another rich nigga to attach they leaching-ass lips to. Know how to play the game, that's all I'm saying. It would make the world a happier place.

For the record, just to make sure we all are clear about everything, I was never with Malcolm because he had money. I was working the hell out of my master's degree in communication, and was eating very high on the hog when me and Malcolm hooked up. That's why he knew that I only expected the very best from him. I didn't need Malcolm for material shit. I could buy that myself. That was just one of the perks that being married to Malcolm afforded me. Private school for the kids and the whole nine.

The night we got married I told Malcolm that I wasn't taking any shit from him. No, I didn't tell him I would chop his ass up into little pieces if I found out he cheated, but I did warn him that he might not want to go there with me. I made it very clear what I expected from him and I thought he understood. Maybe I gave him too much credit.

"Malcolm, are you sure this is what you want?" I asked him as we lay intertwined in the middle of a king-sized bed in a suite on the top floor of the Delaware Avenue Hyatt. We had been chilling there since our trip to the justice of the peace in downtown Philadelphia, where my best friend and a friend of his witnessed the ceremony We couldn't leave for a honeymoon just yet because Malcolm had a lot of business he needed to tie up, and I had to make moves at work as well to ensure time off.

"Babe, I've never wanted this with anyone else. I promise you this is what we were made for."

"Yeah?" I asked him with a skeptical look on my face.

"Yeah," he responded, sounding sure.

"Okay. Just so you know, you fuck with me you stuck with me. I don't believe in divorce."

"There's no need to. This is a forever thing. Now get over her on daddy's dick and show me what I can expect from Mrs. Malcolm Bernard."

I climbed on top of that stallion and put in work. I hoped that he wasn't going to fuck it up, and that it would last forever. He had me fooled for quite a few years that everything was on point and that we were cool. Malcolm and I didn't argue all the time. He wasn't beating the shit out of me, or anything like that. We actually had a very open relationship, and we got along really well. Never in my wildest dreams did I think that Malcolm would set me up to be hurt, but just like most cheating men he started getting sloppy and the evidence started to show.

As I began to circle the Midlothian, Virginia neighborhood I was just as impressed at the area. The homes on Robious Road looked new, and expensive. Two things I knew Malcolm loved. The houses were gorgeous and spoke volumes about the amount of money people paid to live in those parts. It was already broad daylight, so I couldn't make any moves just yet, and was actually on my way to the hotel I would be staying at, but I wanted to get a feel for where I would be going once the day was over and it was dark. This trip was going to be a little different than the others, and I couldn't wait to get it over with.

I already had a rental car set up and ready to go for me near the hotel that I would be staying at. I didn't want to drive my truck around here because I didn't want to risk it being connected to the drops I had already made. So far it was still up in the air about who had done the insanely crazy drop-off at the first house, but I knew that it was only a matter of time before the dots started to connect. I also planned to leave my truck at this hotel. One of the last two bags leaked horribly in the back and there was dried blood and fluid everywhere. I knew once they searched the truck it would be over, but even then they would still have to catch up to me.

The only room that I was concerned about them catching me in was the last room on the stop. That was where I was supposed to be caught. If you haven't noticed, women never get caught by surprise. If you catch a woman cheating, lying, stealing, and doing anything they are not supposed to be doing it's because they wanted to get caught. We are too smooth to get caught up, and can keep secrets for years. On some real shit I could have offed Malcolm's ass and buried his body in the backyard, reported him missing, and would have gotten away with it for years without the police knowing. I would have built a rose garden right over his dead remains. What I did with him was personal, and all of these women needed to know that I was one not to be fucked with. Crossing me was not a good move. If you didn't know, now you do.

This last chick had me almost salivating because I couldn't wait to get her ass back. This one was the most personal of them all. Seeing her with Malcolm was really the reason behind what I done. I knew about the other women . . . almost expected it because a man is going to be a man. This one right here, though, she played dirty. We were close, and I thought I could confide in her.

All of us have that one person we can call at three in the morning to vent when we couldn't find anyone else to tell our business to. You know, that person who is supposed to take everything you say to the grave. The one who will put you right in your place if you are wrong, and when you are right will ride to the death of it all with you. The one person in the world besides your momma you can count on for anything, when all of your motor skills are nonexistent, and one and one are no longer adding up to two. Your road dog, your sound mind, your peace when you can't find any anywhere else. When that person betrays you it's almost like the world comes to a halt and you can't function.

I thought someone had knocked the life out of me when the private investigator showed me the last set of pictures that he gathered on my cheating-ass husband. He dropped off a thick envelope filled to the max with photos of various women, and most of them I skipped through because it really just looked like my husband was being flirtatious. As the photos went on I had to pause for a second because I didn't believe what I was seeing. Holding each photo close to my face I had to blink a few times to clear my vision. Was I really seeing what I was seeing?

Pictures of my asshole husband naked on her deck, in the Jacuzzi, in the living, dining, and kitchen area, the backyard and more were in the pile. There were photos of him and her on a yacht, holding hands in restaurants, and walking out in public. They even managed to have picnics in this indoor garden that I had been dying to get to but he never had time. They looked like they were in love . . . they looked like they were enjoying their lives together . . . they looked like they didn't have a care in the world.

I dropped the pictures back into the pile, not sure who I had to deal with first. All of the phone calls and the late-night talks, and all of the "girl, you have to work it out, he's a good man" speeches that I sat through. She convinced me that I was just being paranoid and that Malcolm was a good man.

"I'll keep an eye on him when he's down this way. You know I'm not letting no man mess over my family," my first cousin spoke into the phone, sounding pissed that Malcolm had hurt me again. Our mothers were sisters, and we grew up close like sisters as children. When she moved to Virginia I was so sad that she was so far away, but I was excited that she had found a house, and we made plans for me to visit soon.

"I can't come visit, cousin. I'm glad you finally got the money up for the house," I spoke to her, genuinely happy that she had found a place for her and the kids to live.

"Girl, I had to suck a lot of dick to get this house." She laughed into the phone. "But it's beautiful, and I can't wait for you to see it. Now let me get these kids to bed. Tell Malcolm I said hey, and I hope to see you all soon!"

We said our good-byes, and that was it. We talked

almost every day about the shit I was going through with him, and how I was still trying to make a name for myself in the TV industry. She rode for me the entire time, and often told me how she bragged about having a famous cousin on the tube. We were best friends, and I trusted her with my life. Out of all the people in the world she was the last one I expected to be fucking my husband, and for that reason she had to be taught a lesson as well. Don't betray your family. We are all you have.

I played it cool though. You would be proud of me. When I called her and told her that I would be coming up to visit she was hype, and made plans to get rid of the kids. The night I killed Malcolm I made sure after he was all bagged up to call her and let her know that we were driving down. I told her that I would be stopping through first, and Malcolm would be coming later because he had business to take care of. She sent her kids to their dad's house, and even let me know that she had done a little shopping and would be cooking me dinner.

"That's perfect, Sherae! Can't wait to see you. We will be heading out early to beat traffic. Make sure you have dinner ready because I know I will be hungry."

I was irked that she was still being as fake as she was. She fucked my man. The ultimate betrayal in my book, but she was about to get the same thing he got. A nice dirt nap.

"Hey, cousin, I'm in town. I'll be over there in a few hours. Can't wait to see you," I said to her after I got my rental and was comfortable at the hotel.

"Girl, I have a feast waiting for us. The kids are gone and I'm ready to get turned up!"

"Me too! See you in a few!"

We disconnected our call, and I made my way into the bathroom so that I could come out of this diaper and take a nice bath. After that I made sure that I still had the supply of the same meds I killed Malcolm with ground up in a small vial in my wallet. I got cute and ready to see my cousin. I decided to go ahead and drive my truck to my cousin's because she would want to know why I got a rental car. Plus the rest of my husband was in the truck and it would just be easier to transport him in it.

As I said, out of all of them she definitely hurt me the most, so she would get it just like he did. Family or not, betrayal is betrayal. I was going to enjoy this one though. This was the snake who smiled in my face and dug her fangs in my back when it was turned. I couldn't wait to see the look on her face when she realized she was going to die. This was going to be bittersweet, but it had to happen. I really didn't have a choice in the matter. Both she and Malcolm chose their fate. That's my story, and I was sticking to it.

21

Payback from Way Back

When I pulled into her driveway I parked the truck and got out, making my way up to her door. Before I could even ring the bell she had flung the door open and pulled me into the tightest embrace ever like she really missed me. I wanted to ask her if she hugged my husband the same way when he was over here, but I refrained from any questioning. She wasn't supposed to know this early that I knew, but I had the photos and she would get the pleasure of looking at some of them before she died. It took everything in me not to wrap around her conniving ass like a cobra and squeeze the life out of her, but I refrained. My reward would be coming soon enough.

"Girl, I am so glad you are here." She smiled at me as she hugged me again, afterward giving me a tour of her house. The dumb shit was decorated almost like mine, which meant to me that when Malcolm was getting shit for our house he was buying one for her as well. I needed an Oscar for the performance I put on as I fawned over the shit she had that looked just like mine but may have been in a different color. Another wanna-be-me bitch to add to the list. I hated that she was family, but that was how it all went down.

"Dinner is going to be off the chain. I already have the table set. Pour us a few glasses of wine so that we can get started. I'm going to take off my work clothes and get comfy so we can catch up," she explained. This was working better than I thought. You have to know that the minute she was gone I took the liberty of fixing our plates and lacing everything I gave her with the drug. She made this real easy for me, and I almost felt bad for doing it. Almost. She betrayed me, and I kept repeating that in my head so that I wouldn't talk myself out of it. By the time she got back I was sitting down enjoying a glass of wine. I was getting myself tipsy waiting for the show to start. This was the best part because it wasn't expected.

"Your house is beautiful, honey," I complimented her as she sat and made herself comfy. I wanted to tell her that it was a cheap replica of mine, but it didn't matter. Might as well let her be great while she can. The photos I had of her and my husband were in my bag, and I couldn't wait for the right time to pull them out.

"Thank you, dear. Most of the stuff is gifts," she admitted as she downed her first glass of wine and poured another. "I had to do some strange shit for some of this stuff, but it was well worth it. What's going on with you? When is Malcolm showing up? I haven't seen you guys in so long."

I almost jumped across the table after she told that bald-faced lie. The pictures from the private investigator showed a time stamp on a few of the pictures showing a date from just a few days ago. The night that Malcolm came home with the lipstick on the collar smelling like some other bitch. Come to find out the other bitch was family. Gotta love them, right?

"He's not that far from here and will be here soon. I'm starving though, so let's eat!"

I dug into my plate because I truly was hungry as hell. I hadn't really eaten anything besides that dry-ass breakfast I had at the hotel the other day. I'd really just been living off the little bit of food I had packed when I left

Philly, and had been sleeping mostly in between drop-off points. I figured I might as well enjoy my last meal while I had the chance. Wasn't no use in being hungry if I didn't have to be, you dig?

She was really chatting it up as she dug into her plate as well. I mixed the same drug I gave my husband with ground-up Tylenol 3. Five of them to be exact. She was going to die from the deadly dose of Prolixin anyway, but I was hoping the Tylenol 3 would make her feel sleepy first before everything else jumped off. I didn't think I could watch my cousin die the same way I watched everyone else because regardless of everything we were family, but it was already in motion. I sprinkled some in the mashed potatoes, the gravy of the meatloaf, and mixed it in the salad dressing before dressing her salad with it. After pouring my glass of wine, I laced her glass, and poured a healthy amount of the drug in the wine bottle, because if I knew my cousin she would be having more than one glass this evening.

"I'm so glad you were able to make it down here. I miss being around y'all more often. Have you thought of relocating down this way? You could do your segment from anywhere, I'm sure," she babbled on as she devoured her plate and sucked down the contents of her glass.

"We've talked about it a few times because Malcolm does a lot of women . . . I mean, a lot of business down here," I replied, catching my slip-up. She didn't seem to notice as she continued to run her mouth and eat from her plate. I was wondering if I had put enough of the drug in her food because it felt like it was taking longer to take effect than it did with Malcolm. I would hate to have to shoot her, but she was going to die tonight either way. Pretty soon I could see her eyes starting to look heavy, and it was getting harder for her to keep her head up on her shoulders.

"Oh my, I didn't realize how tired I was." She yawned as her eyes started to look like they were too heavy to keep up.

"Yeah, it's like that when you are spending all your time fucking other people's husbands for material shit," I said calmly as I continued to enjoy my plate.

The look on her face was priceless as she tried to keep her head up. She looked like she wanted to deny it, but she couldn't even get her thoughts together from the effects of the drugs. I took the liberty of retrieving the photos from my bag so that she could see them before she rolled out. This part I was going to enjoy the most. I couldn't stand for a person to lie with the evidence right in front of them. She was getting real drowsy so it was time to let the show begin.

"This picture is of you fucking my husband in your bedroom," I spoke to her as I placed the photos down on her plate. I could see she was trying to focus but was having trouble.

"In these y'all were in the bathroom, kitchen, living area, and on this very dining room table. I guess y'all were christening this new house he helped you buy and furnish. It looks just like mine on the inside but cheaper, and not nearly as clean."

She looked like she wanted to try to explain herself but she couldn't get it together. I could see the slight tremor her body started to get, so I knew the Prolixin was starting to work. It was time to really move into the next phase.

"Wait, favorite cousin, I think Malcolm is here now. I'll be right back!"

She was sitting back in her chair with her eyes the size of saucers as she tried to catch her breath and get her bearings. I went outside and gathered the last of the bags up to bring in. Placing them by the table, I put on the surgical gloves I had been wearing and searched through the bags until I found the one I was looking for. Reaching inside I pulled out Malcolm's bloody head and placed it right in front of her so that they could look at each other.

"Here he is, boo. The man you were in love with. The one you could never give me any real details about, but you knew you loved him. It was complicated, you said. He had a situation but y'all were working it out is what you told me. It's a shame that you forgot to tell me I was the situation. Shame on you for lying to me, honey."

"You . . . are going . . . to . . ." she managed to get out before going into a coughing fit. I offered her the poisoned glass to help her swallow it down. "You are going to rot in hell for this."

"I'll meet you there in a bathing suit. I hear it's pretty hot down there this time of year."

I took my seat on the other side of the table and watched the drugs take effect. I thought I was going to feel bad but I was truly enjoying the show as she coughed and gargled, gagging on her own saliva as her tongue began to swell. I took the liberty of finishing my plate as she slid from the chair and began to flop around on the floor like a fish out of water. She definitely got what she deserved, and in my opinion she was lucky I picked this way to let her go and I didn't decide to torture her. We were family. I hated that Malcolm cheated on me with any woman, but we grew up like sisters and it hurt the most that she would betray me like this.

By the time I came back from raiding the kitchen with a bowl of ice cream she was lying on her side, nearly under the table, foaming at the mouth. This actually happened a lot faster than I thought it would, and I was sure it was because I nearly quadrupled the dose that would take her out.

I enjoyed my dessert and checked my Facebook status until I was sure she was gone. I resisted the urge to stomp her simply because she was already dead so it wouldn't matter. I was relieved that I actually handled the entire situation without being caught, and I decided that maybe instead of going farther south I would put another plan in motion.

My first thought was to leave a bloody mess like I did at all the other houses, but it didn't matter at this point. I served her Malcolm's head on a platter. I was done with this scene. Leaving everything the way it was I gathered my purse and car keys and I left. Hopefully her parents would have fun planning her funeral. Too bad I wouldn't be there for it.

22

Am I Worth It

By the time I got back to my hotel room I was exhausted. There were a lot of emotions and thoughts swimming through my head that had me overwhelmed. I didn't have any regrets by far, I was just worried what would happen to my kids after all of this was said and done. I didn't want them to have to go through life with people pointing an accusatory finger at them like they should have to pay for the mistakes their parents made. Neither of them asked to be here, and in reality it really wasn't fair to them.

This was a hell of a time to be thinking about all of this, but what was done was done. I took a seat on the bed and thought about everything that had happened in my life. I was pretty successful and had made a name for myself. Too bad by the time this was over no one would remember all of that. I would be going down in history as the woman who killed her husband and spread his body parts across the South. It was almost funny to me, but not quite. Maybe I am as crazy as people will think I am once they've learned of what I have done.

I couldn't sleep so I decided to head back toward Philadelphia. Maybe I would turn myself in once I got there. No one knew I had done all of these heinous things yet, so maybe I could go back to my life. I quickly retracted the thought. There was nothing normal about my life anymore. The man I loved was gone, and I was a murderer.

I couldn't provide a stable house for my children like this so what did I have to really go back to?

As I drove throughout the night I thought about Malcolm and all the memories we had. Some made me laugh out loud, and some made me cry uncontrollably and I had to actually pull to the side of the road to get my life before moving on. Maybe I could go and say good-bye to my kids once more before they locked me up. After this shit I was sure they would be giving me the death penalty anyway.

A few hours later I pull up to the beginning of the Chesapeake Bay Bridge. It is beautiful at night with all the lights that trail the length of the bridge. The lights go on for miles, and in the dark you can see where the bridge goes underwater where it turns into a tunnel because those spaces in the water are dark. The Chesapeake is a pretty lengthy ride and in the daytime the water looks so close it feel like you can put your arm right out the car window and drag your fingers through it. I used to be so afraid to drive across the Chesapeake because once you are on it there is no turning back, and all there is on either side is water. It looks like never-ending ocean out here, and it is so peaceful. I just sit on the side, right at the entrance of the bridge, with the radio playing on a late-night slow jams station. Every song that the deejay plays reminds me of a different time in my life with Malcolm.

"'What would you give and what would it take for you to show me that I'm worth all the love . . .'" I sing along to the vocals of Heather Headley, wondering that very same thing. *Am I worth it? If I had kept him around what would I have had to do to show him I was worth all of his time and attention and that he didn't need all of those other women?* This shit brings me to tears and I hate feeling weak.

Reaching into my bag I find the bottle containing the Vicodin that I brought from the house. I have seven pills left in the bottle, and before I can change my mind I start popping them back, chased with a bottle of wine that I took from my cousin's house. It is one of those situations where I don't see the need to even be around anymore. Besides my kids, no one else matters, and I am okay with dying right now. As song after song plays I not only go through my supply of Vicodin, I also toss back the last of the Tylenol 3 that I have at the bottom of my bag. There will be no pain when I leave here, and that in itself puts a smile on my face.

I start to just sit here and let the medicine take me in an overdose, but I don't want it to be that easy. Before I can talk myself out of it I start my car and begin to drive the length of the bridge at full speed. I haven't seen a car pass in a while so I know there is no one in front of me who I can put in danger. I want to get to the deepest part of the bay so that I can't be found hopefully for days. Rolling the windows up as the lines on the road start to blur, I know that it is almost time.

When I come out of the last tunnel I count backward from five. In my head I ask God and my kids for forgiveness just as I sharply turn my car to the right, causing my truck to jump the guard rail and plunge into the water, causing a huge splash. It is pitch black out here, and no one is around, so there will be no one to save me from my watery grave. Some will say I deserve to be here after all I have done, and I probably do. I am just glad it is over and done with.

As my car begins to sink into the water I can feel the ice-cold water rushing in around my feet as darkness closes in around me. All I can remember is how nice the lights on the bridge look at night as the meds finally overtake me and I can't keep my eyes open any longer. I lay my head on the headrest as my body responds to the shock from the water and the lethal dose of medication I took. I am gone before the car reaches the bottom and the water has a chance to completely submerge me in the car. It will be days before they find me, and the letters I left to my kids in the trunk of the truck. This will be my legacy, and hopefully every mistress who hears my story will learn to keep their pussies to themselves after this. A lesson is to be learned from this, but how many will get it is beyond me. This is Te'Nae at ten signing out . . . good day and good riddance!

Part Three

Shay and Justin

—Chrisette Michele, "Goodbye Game"

23

Shay

"Earlier today the body of our beloved weather girl, and host of the popular morning show *Te'Nae at Ten,* was found at the bottom of the Chesapeake Bay, this after the gruesome discovery of some of her husband's remains reportedly found scattered along the East Coast in several areas south of Philadelphia. It has not been said if she had anything to do with the murder of her husband, CEO Malcolm Bernard, a mogul in the music and film industries, but it was reported that they were supposed to be on vacation. It appears that Mrs. Bernard may have driven her vehicle off the bridge on purpose as she was found at the bottom of the bay still buckled into her seat. More to come after this brief commercial break. . . ."

My mouth was wide open as I listened to the morning news. I had to pause for a second from getting dressed because I couldn't believe what I just heard. Not that I knew the newscaster personally, but I definitely tuned in every morning to listen to her weather forecast as I got myself together to get ready to go. I loved her on the screen, and wished every day that my husband would let me get just a little plastic surgery so that I could look just like her. She was fierce! Hair always perfect and eyebrows to die for. A lot of people often told me that we looked like we could be related, and I saw it too. I was tempted to just go and get some shit done and deal with his mess later, but I didn't feel like the bullshit that would come with it.

Hell, who was I fooling? Justin didn't make enough money for us to do shit but pay bills. Let me recap that . . . we made good money. He just didn't want to spend it on anything but bills and stupid shit for his car. He kept talking this he wanted a baby shit, but he couldn't even take care of himself. How in hell was he going to be responsible for a whole other person? His pipe dream was what sucked me in. I believed that we could be a power couple, but all we turned into was a couple who fought and fussed all the damn time. This after spending damn near $30,000 on a wedding that he couldn't even come up with half the money for. I blamed myself for that because he kept trying to scale it down. I wasn't trying to hear it though. I did everything on a grand scale, and this fool just couldn't keep up.

I refused to let him make us look like we couldn't afford shit. He always complained about me trying to keep up with the Jones's . . . whoever they were. I had to remind him that I wasn't trying to keep up with shit. Everyone was having trouble keeping up with me. I made sure I kept "us" fly because he wasn't about to embarrass me. Damn that! I had an image to uphold, and my family was not about to see that I was possibly on the brink of falling off. Not Shay Michaels . . . lead diva supreme. It would be a cold day in hell if I ever got to the bottom.

Okay, maybe I was being a little harsh. Justin made good money . . . damn good money. He wasn't CEO of a corporation or anything, but he did own his own tow truck company that was pulling in crazy dollars, and he had four auto collision shops spread around Philly that pulled in mad dough as well. So, don't get it fucked up. My man had money . . . he just wasn't as polished as I wanted him to be.

When I first met him I was smitten by the handsome grease monkey who had come to save me. I had gotten sideswiped on my way to work by some fool who was acting like he was going to pull off without giving me his information. He jumped out of his lane and smacked my car into an entirely different lane and made me hit another car. Of course all either of the other cars had was bumper damage, but my car was sitting there, undrivable, looking like a pile of Lego pieces. I was *heated!* Then the dude who hit me had the nerve to curse me out like I did something wrong. By the time the police got there they damn near had to peel me off of him.

At any rate, Justin was like a superhero when he got there. He pulled me to the side to see if I was okay, and wiped the tears from my face. We sat down in my mangled car, and he told me I had nothing to worry about as he dispatched a tow truck to come pick up what was left of my BMW. As I filled out the paperwork to allow him to move my car, he comforted me, giving me a business card with his number on the back. He instructed me to write my number down on the slip so that they would know how to contact me at the shop, and told his crew that they should put down the deposit for my rental so that I could get on with my day. A boss. I loved his take-charge demeanor and his no-nonsense attitude. Even the cops respected him, and they checked with him to see if he was good as they did what they had to do.

I was smitten, but dismissed him because he wasn't the caliber of man I dated. I did the suit-and-tie, power-lunch type of men. Not these wreck-chasing hood dudes. They just weren't my speed. Still, there was something about him that pulled on my clit a little, and I was considering taking him for a test drive. Maybe there was something under the layers of motor oil that I could turn into a mogul.

It took a few days, but he actually called me to see how things were going. The day of the accident was like a blur, but the guys at the shop definitely took care of me and I reported that to him when he called. I was trying to make the conversation quick, but Mr. Flirtatious was not letting me off the phone that easy. Like I said, he wasn't the type of man I went for, but there was no harm in lunch right? I just hoped he knew I wasn't a McDonald's drive-through kind of girl. Lunch at Ms. Tootsie's would do just fine.

Who knew that lunch would turn into a late night and early morning? I certainly didn't. I wasn't planning to take this thing further than a few crab mac-and-cheese balls and a sweet tea from Ms. Tootsie's, but he made me forget that he even showed up in a dirty jumper with his hat turned to the back. I don't know what I was expecting, but when I pulled up at the restaurant and parked I almost walked right past him. Justin really knew how to clean up. I mean, he wasn't Gucci down to the socks, but he was Sean John fresh, and he smelled delicious. The scent of his Dolce & Gabbana tickled my nose in a good way, and I must say that it definitely scored him some cool points.

Lunch was light and breezy. We laughed. We flirted. I took him home and fucked him good, sending him on his way with a smile on his face afterward. Hell, I needed it and it was good. It had been awhile since I had gotten dick worth bragging about and of course I couldn't wait to tell my homegirl about it. That day turned into another date and a few more nights, and pretty soon we were seeing each other on a consistent basis. Still, he wasn't the caliber of man I wanted to really be seen with, so I played with powerbrokers and men who cashed checks for hundreds of thousands during the day, and at night I gave my body up for some thug loving that I couldn't get enough of.

Don't ask me how it happened, but one day I realized that I more than liked Justin. Not gonna say that I loved him at that point, but I was definitely digging him. I mean, every moment I wasn't working I was with him. We even started going out in the daytime. Not in the city where someone I knew could see me, but we did take day trips to museums, and things of that nature. It surprised me how much he knew about art, and textures, and I was certain that he had missed his calling. I assumed that maybe he just needed direction to reach his full potential, and a part of me was okay with that. A very small part, but I liked a man who was comfortable in his skin.

Throwing caution to the wind I decided to take a chance on something different and see what Justin was capable of. Prince Charming doesn't always show up on a horse dressed as a knight in shining armor. Sometimes he comes disguised as something totally unexpected and not all shiny and new. It was up to me to decide if I was going to miss out on happiness to please everyone, or if I was going to finally do what was best for me. Stepping out on luck, I decided to dive in heart first and give this thing a try. That was the best and the worst decision I ever made in my life. Too bad I didn't find out why until way later on.

24

Shay

I had been told many times that I was an enabler. I fed into people's weaknesses with this take-charge attitude that I hid behind, and because I could never let people do things for themselves they solely depended on me to make things right and therefore never did shit for themselves. Let's be real, whether someone comes up with what they owe you or not at the end of the day shit had to be paid. If that person didn't have their half that didn't mean that you didn't still owe. That's what being an adult is about. We stress all hard to be able to do what we want only to have to get jobs to pay for all the shit we have to have but really don't need. It's supposed to be a little easier when you have a partner, but when that partner is not on the same page you are on, things can go haywire, and then the turmoil begins. So I fixed things. That's what I did; I was a fixer. That's the biggest part of the problem.

In the beginning Justin spared no expense on the things he wanted to do for me. Come to find out my greasy little mechanic drove a hot little BMW as well, and although he didn't live on the Main Line, he was living pretty well in Bala Cynwood, and his place was very nice. It made me look at him in a different light, and I had a deeper appreciation of what he was capable of. The thing about people you always have to remember is they will pay for things they want, but neglect the necessities. He had me with the car, and the watches, and even the dates to restaurants I'd never heard of before, but when it came to taking care of home it was always an issue with him.

Happy wife, happy life . . . you've heard the saying I'm sure. Believe that there's truth in it. I was a happy wife with a happy life at one point and I was still trying to figure out when the script had been flipped. Was it the first time I decided to look in his phone only to find texts and pictures from some random bitch he denied having feelings for? Maybe, but the way I saw it was we all share everybody whether we do it willingly or it is unbeknownst to you. No one was faithful, and even if you did everything there was always someone out there doing it better. It's up to you to decide whether you were going to stay, and I did, but it's up to you whether you are going to be able to live with that uncomfortable feeling for the duration of your relationship.

What feeling? You know the one you get the moment he doesn't answer his phone, or the minute he is late from work. Or the midday call that goes unanswered and you wonder for five seconds if he's out creeping with some raggedy bitch because surely she wouldn't be as fly as you. I had all of these doubts and thoughts in my head because my husband was a superhero for a living. He came to the rescue for women all day long who had been hurt in one wreck or another, and just like he charmed his way into my bed, I was sure it was just as easy to do the same with someone else.

I hated playing Inspector Gadget. It took too much time and energy, but sometimes you just had to take a look and see how green the grass on the other side was. Like I said, I had an image to uphold, and I couldn't have people thinking that my household wasn't in order. Truth be told, something had been up with my significant other for a while, and I was just getting tired of the mood swings.

My husband left one of his phones home one morning. Normally I didn't even bother looking through them because he had about three phones that he used for business, and most of the time the call log was jammed with numbers with no names attached because they belonged to people who had cars at his collision shops. It was no big deal to me. People had the right to call about their vehicles. The phones buzzed all day long most days, and I just allowed him to be great because that's how he made his money.

On this day it was like the phone had a weird glow about it. Like it was beckoning me to search it. None of the phones had pass codes on them, so it wasn't like I would have to bust out the safecracker to get it in. It was just a feeling that I got that maybe I should see what was going on. I convinced myself that it was harmless to take a look. After all, there was nothing incriminating in the phone, right? I mean, if there was I was sure he would be smart enough to erase it. These were business phones . . . for business . . . and that's it. When I picked up the phone it felt extra hot in my hands and I almost dropped it.

"This is wrong," I said to myself as I set the phone back down on the counter. Who would cheat on me? I was the truth, and provided for my household in all aspects. There was no way there was someone else out there satisfying my man . . . or was there?

"Okay, I'm just going to take a quick look." I continued the conversation with myself, gripping the phone back up and pressing the button for the home screen.

I started to scroll, but then thought about it. If there was some shit in his phone that I didn't like was I going to leave? There was no use in getting hype if all we were going to do is fuck after the argument and move on to the next day. That was my rationale in my head, but that didn't stop my fingers from pressing the little envelope that held his text messages. I wasn't breathing as the multiple folders popped up on his phone, and at this point there was no turning back it seemed like. I was already in his messages, so I might as well stay committed to checking them out.

I started to breathe a little easier as I opened up each file and saw that they were all texts about business. People checking on the status of their cars, order updates for parts and the like. I actually began to feel silly as I scrolled through. I mean, folks had the right to look into the status of their vehicle. I remembered having called several times while my car was in the shop to see what was up.

Just as I was going to call it a day, I saw a text from someone that looked odd. It was the only number that actually had a name. Not a proper name, but a name nonetheless. Tapping the box, the name caught me off-guard before the contents of the text. The name read 1BDBTCH, but I definitely read between the lines.

Last night was everything. When are you coming back for an encore? the text read to my husband. Wasn't shit slow about me, so I knew instantly that he had tapped that ass and she wanted some more.

I already told you I had a situation. I can't just come through whenever, he replied. I was floored. As much as I did for him and this fool was stepping out? *You have got to be kidding me.*

I know, boo, but I don't know how long I'll be able to wait for you to come back. You got me open. My legs and my heart. I love you, Calvin, she responded. My hands were starting to shake, and I could feel myself starting to sweat. I wanted to put the phone down but I couldn't. It was like I was trying to avoid a collision, but my brakes stopped working.

Who the fuck is Calvin? Not only was this ungrateful

fool stepping out, but he was giving bitches a fake name? Who the hell was I sleeping next to every night? I put the phone back down on the counter as my body turned numb. I could feel my heart turning into ice by the second, and I hated the way it felt. I was going to confront Justin about this, but at the right time. I was going to give him enough rope to hang himself, and was definitely going to enjoy kicking the chair from under him so that he could hang himself. After calling out from work, I put my plan into action. Justin was going to pay for ever cheating on me, and he was not going to like the outcome.

25

Justin

I could pull any chick I wanted. Especially after a collision. They were at their most vulnerable at that point, and would take just about anything anyone had to offer. Not that I was into using people, so don't get that impression, but women especially really feel safe with a man with a tow truck. When we show up that means that they are no longer stranded and they feel a sense of safety. We all have an S on our chest whether we want it there or not.

I had bedded plenty of the women I came to help, but when I met Shay there was a different vibe I got from her. She didn't strike me as the type who needed saving. In fact, I had to get her to simmer down because she was all over the guy who hit her like she wanted to kill him. I could see why though. She drove a nice, slick BMW F30 and the guy who hit her was pushing an old-ass Ford pickup that knocked her clear across the street. She had every reason to be upset, and on the low that shit had me open. Too often we had to wear the cape, but it was nice to see a sista handling her business the way she was.

I never thought we would end up down the aisle. Everything about Shay screamed money. From the Gucci briefcase that dangled from her well-manicured nails down to the red-bottom Christian Louboutins that covered her feet. She was well put together, but there was a little hood under all that shine that kept her down to earth. That's what I liked about her immediately. Even when the truck came, she didn't cringe at the thought of riding in filth. She simply hiked her dress up, and climbed in even after I offered to drive her in my car.

"Honey, you got money to make. Go ahead and get yours. I'll be fine, and thanks again for your help."

A woman after my own heart. I didn't think that she would call me, and once a few days had gone by and I hadn't heard from her I gave her a buzz. As polished as she was, I really wasn't that far out of her league. I came from having a criminal background to having a lucrative business in just under a year. I knew when I got locked up that jail was not the place for me, and the minute I got out I was on my grind to open my first shop. That turned into three more shops just two years later, and I had been rolling ever since.

I had money . . . plenty of it, and it was all legit. So it was nothing for me to take Shay to a nice restaurant where there wasn't a drive-through and a cartoon clown mascot. Of course I didn't let on what I was rolling with, not that I think it would matter to her. She definitely had her own, so I wasn't worried about her digging in my pockets. I was even more surprised when she gave up the yams on the first date, but like she said, there wasn't any use in waiting to be disappointed. That just made me like her even more. She was real upfront with her situation, and in what she believed. I was cool with all of that.

Shay was bossy though. And after a while that started to grate on my nerves. It was Shay's way or no way. Once we got married she was always on my top, and not in a good way. She was more of a pain in the ass now, and sometimes a man just needed some peace. It was way too easy to find replacements. I ran across them every day all day, but this last chick I ran into got me caught up for real, and if I wasn't careful she could really mess around and fuck shit up for me home. Shay is a lunatic, and I would hate for them two to cross paths.

Let's be honest for a second. Men can cheat all day long every day, but I promise you if I ever caught wind of Shay stepping out I would have gone clean off. I didn't play all the time, and although I was caught up in some shit right now, she just better have been on her game. I was trying to let it go, but this other chick was one bad bitch, and that's exactly how I had her stored in my phone. She was another polished gem I ran across in a collision, and I just had a fetish for women who were well put together. When I say a body to die for? Lord, I was well into my grave when I saw all those curves get out of her damaged car, and I had to get my thoughts together before stepping to her about the accident. She was no Shay though; she was well composed and very understanding of the situation and even asked the guy who hit her if he was okay.

She was very cooperative with the exchange of information, and when I offered her a ride in my car instead of the tow truck she gladly accepted, joking that she didn't want to smudge her new Michael Kors dress. I opened up the car door and tucked her away for safe keeping as I instructed my crew on where to take her car, which was a closer location to her house, and to get her rental ready to rock. It was supposed to be a drop-off and I was going to keep it pushing, but when she insisted on letting her take me to dinner I couldn't tell her no. She had her hooks in me, and when her pillow-soft lips landed damn near on mine when I pulled up to the rental location I knew I should get as far away from her as I could. Too bad I didn't listen to my own advice.

She was the toxic type. Dangerous in her own right. She didn't give a flying rat's ass that I was married because so was she. Her logic was that it all canceled each other out so it wasn't considered cheating; it was more like sharing.

What our spouses didn't know wouldn't hurt us, and telling on me would be telling on herself. That was her theory.

"Don't worry, love. Your secret is safe with me," she whispered in my ear one night as she rode me down into the bed. She gave out toe-curling blow jobs that had me amazed every time, and she sponsored the entire affair. Every time we met up at a hotel, motel, or Holiday Inn it was on her dime. She always had everything on point, and each room came complete with champagne and chocolate-covered strawberries. She spoiled me, and I quickly forgot that I had to handle my business at home to keep Shay happy as well.

Things did start to get a little hectic as my mistress demanded more of my time, but Shay seemed to be pulling further away so it kind of made it easier to accommodate the other woman. Being a typical male, I didn't even realize I was getting sloppy with my shit, but I knew I had to do something before the cat was entirely out of the bag. The first thing I needed to do was find my cell phone. The things she would find in there alone would be enough for her to send my ass packing and take everything I had with me. We didn't sign a prenuptial agreement when we got married, so I knew Shay would take me for everything. My simple ass opened up my mouth and told her I wanted a baby, which further dug my grave. If I was going to be a family man I needed to let go of this situation I was in and focus. It was just so damn good, and the more I met up with her the harder it was for me to step off.

"Michelle, we can't keep doing this. What if your husband finds out? What if my wife finds out?" I asked her on afternoon as we were getting cleaned up from a lunchtime rendezvous. She had this thing where she liked to get fucked on her lunch breaks. I had a crew of twenty men chasing wrecks so I wasn't worried about losing any money, especially since it only took about two hours out of my day to hook up with her. It's just that I could feel her starting to get clingy again, and sometimes I had to gently remind her that we both had significant others.

"Of course we can. I'm good to you, right?" she asked as she reached into my unbuckled pants with her warm hands, getting me all riled up again. All she had to do was touch me with her pinky finger and I would be ready to go.

"You are great, but don't you think we should slow down some? Maybe show your husband the attention you show me," I suggested as I regrettably pulled her hand from my pants so that I could button them.

"My husband gets sucked and fucked every night, so don't worry about him. It appears that your wife is the one who needs to step her game up," she snapped back with a cockiness that shut me up. That shit turned me on something serious. "I'll call you in a few days. That should give you enough time to get your home situation together. Be ready to rock, and leave your apprehension at the door. It spoils the mood."

And with that she strutted her sexy ass right out of the hotel door. I always gave her a few minutes to get ghost before I came out behind her so that no one would see us leaving together. Her husband was some big shot CEO of a major marketing firm, and she was always very watchful of his colleagues being in the area. She wasn't about to fuck up her money either, and I wasn't mad at her about that.

Once the coast was clear I made my way out and headed to my shop on West Oak Lane. I had to get away from this area for a while so that I could think. Michelle brought it to my attention that I wasn't getting enough attention at home. Before now I didn't even think about it, and that bothered me a little. Shay was usually very attentive, and if she wasn't giving her attention to me who was she giving it to? I hoped like hell that I wouldn't have to break some dude's face, but then I had to pump my brakes for a second. That was guilt talking because I was out here riding dirty. Shay was probably just busy with one of her projects at work, and when it got like that she had to put in long hours, and was tired most nights. Michelle had me bugging, and I needed to clear my conscience before I got home.

Before you go judging me, know that I loved my wife and I took our vows seriously. Shay was everything to me. I thought we just lost our way along the way, and maybe we got a little too comfortable with our situation. At one point we were rocking the bed every single night, and most mornings. Shay was the dick-suck queen, and could get me to bust in record time. Every night turned into every other night, which turned into every other week, to once whenever we were home at the same time and the mood hit us.

Shit, if Shay was in her job I probably wouldn't have been out here letting Michelle blow me away every chance she got. Hell, who was I kidding? Yes, I would. Just probably not as often, and I would definitely have more control of the situation. At any rate, I needed to figure this shit out . . . as soon as I found my phone.

26

Shay

The thing men should understand is this: if you want to play the cheating game be prepared to possibly lose. Women are too good at this shit. We could step out of the relationship and have a whole other situation for years and still maintain both sides of the fence without skipping a beat. That's what we do. We are the keeper of secrets, and the best that ever done it. It is a no-win situation, fellas, so be sure that's what you want when you cross that line. Once the line is drawn it's war, and we will play the game and fight until the very end.

I was hurt by Justin, but not surprised. After all, he was a man at the end of the day and in my head the only man in the world who ever stayed faithful was Jesus Christ. Every man besides him, even Adam, was a snake and could not be trusted. My first reaction was to wild out and go ballistic, but I needed to gain from this situation so I kept my cool. *Two can play this game and three can play it better*. It was time for me to start doing me, and I was going to have a ball while I was out here!

Later that day when he came home from work I acted like I had been out at work myself. I had on my sweats and a T-shirt like I normally did when I came home from work, and I had dinner popping in the kitchen. By the time he walked in the door I was putting the finishing touches on some candied yams, and the table was set for two. It had been awhile since we sat and ate dinner, although we vowed after we got married to always engage each other in conversation over dinner every night. Somehow, someway, we stopped doing that, but I was going to show him what he was going to be missing when I was gone. I was going to make him wish he had never stepped foot outside this door, and if he thought what was out there was better they were going to have a big shoe to fill following up behind me.

"Is it my birthday?" he joked as he came into the kitchen. He knew I hated when he walked around the house in his work clothes and I cringed a little as I gritted my teeth to keep from snapping on him.

"No, honey, just dinner. Go ahead and get yourself cleaned up. It's almost done, and I'll have the table set by the time you come back," I responded with a forced smile on my face. He's lucky I wasn't in the business of poisoning people because he would have gotten it today.

He gave me a semi-puzzled look, but I guessed he decided to live in the moment. I turned back to what I was doing, letting him know he was dismissed. This was about to be the ultimate setup, and I was going to slow stroke this one. By the time I dropped the bomb on him his head would be spinning.

While he was in the shower I set our plates, covering them with chrome domes that we got as a wedding gift so that our food could stay warm. I had his favorite wine on ice, and I had a little music playing. Before I forgot, I took the liberty of storing 1BDBTCH's number into my phone so that I could look into that situation as well. I was already on top of everything, but I had to stay in character so that this shit wouldn't bite me in the ass at the end.

Coming out of my sweats, I sat at the table, waiting for my husband in all lace. No underwear was required for this situation because I planned to be dessert. By the time

I would get finished blowing his mind he was going to be useless to any other bitch out there. He would be left with nothing if I could help it, and no real bitch wanted a broke-ass dude. Or did they nowadays?

He came to the table looking and smelling delicious, and I almost forgot that I hated his ass. Justin put the F in fine, honey. I could clearly see why everyone wanted him. From his toasted-almond skin and honey-colored eyes to his precise grooming efforts and buff body . . . Justin was a force to be reckoned with. His pearly white smile drew you right in, and the sound of his voice sent chills down the spines of many. I knew all of this because that's how his crazy ass got me.

"You ready to eat?" I asked him as I pranced around to the other side of the table to pull his chair out. He would be getting the royal treatment tonight. This phase of the game was to get him to let his guard down and upset the others. Guys can't multitask when it comes to cheating, so with all of his attention on me he would surely forget about whoever else was out there for at least a little while. Long enough for me to put my next phase into action.

"Eat you, or what's on the plate?" he asked as he took his seat. He looked like he wanted to start at my toes and work his way up, but we would be playing by my rules tonight, so things would be done my way.

"Your plate, silly. I made us a nice hot meal, so I know you want to get through that."

"Yes, of course. Let's eat."

I tucked his napkin into his robe, right after laying a sloppy wet kiss on his lips. I had to pry his hands from my hips as I released his mouth, and I put an extra dip in my hips as I cat walked back to my seat. The aroma of our food as we removed our covers from our plates made my stomach growl instantly. The smothered turkey chops, candied yams, and fresh garlic string beans looked delectable, and we both dove right in. *Maybe I should have cooked something lighter because this is sure to make us both sleepy.*

"So how has business been?" I asked him as I chowed down on my food. I wanted to hint about him leaving his phone here, but I didn't want him to think that I had gone through it.

"The usual car-after-car scenario. Nothing outside of the ordinary," he replied nonchalantly as he continued to ravish his plate, stopping periodically to wash his food down with a swig of wine.

"Sounds interesting."

"Not really. It's the same stuff, different day. I did misplace one of my phones, and have been looking for it everywhere. Have you seen it?" he asked with a puzzled look on his face. I didn't know how to respond because one of two things could be happening here. Either he really didn't know where his phone was, or he was setting me up for the fall. Against my better judgment I decided to deny that I knew anything.

"No, I haven't seen it. Where did you last have it?"

"I usually kept them all together in the little pouch thing I carry. I'll find it I'm sure," he said as he finished what was left on his plate. "Now, what's for dessert?"

Placing my silverware on my plate, I got up and strutted over to my husband, trying to muster up some feelings to love him again. I was feeling hurt and betrayed, and in my eyes he was a liar. I had to stick to the script though, so I did exactly what was planned.

Moving his plate and place settings out of the way I climbed up on the table and scooted to the edge, draping both of my legs across the arms of his chair. He looked surprised that I didn't have any panties on, and there wasn't an ounce of hair down there. I knew that he liked his yard clean, so I figured I would surprise him with that little treat.

"Dessert is served," I said to him in a seductive tone as I leaned back to watch him feast. It had been a long time since we'd been together like this, and it was too bad that it was all for a setup. He would have to learn to appreciate what he got, and by the time I got done snatching it all away he would be like a lost child in a busy mall trying to find his way back to his mother.

27

Justin

She had my phone. I knew she did, but I would be a fool to ask her for it out right. She probably had already been through it, and saw what was in there. I had a little sense about me, so I never put Michelle's name in the phone, and there was never ever a pic sent or taken of her face from that phone. I didn't need some angry chick calling and blowing up my spot, and I made sure I sent her car to one of my collision shops that was farthest away from the house. Shay never visited the shops outside of the two closest to us, so any pussy action I had going on went across town so that it wouldn't be an issue.

If I played my cards right I could probably keep both of them happy. I was only lunch breaking it with Michelle, but she was starting to act like all of my time belonged to her. Her husband must not have been doing what needed to be done because she was clocking my time like I was a mingling single, and all I had was her. The sex was awesome, but it wasn't good enough to break up my shit at home. She was the side chick. Real plain. Real simple. It was time that she played her position, and I knew just how I had to handle her.

Michelle called for our usual lunch break creep session, but I sent her call to voice mail. She called quite a few times, but I had to show her that she worked on my time, not I on hers. I understood that she worked in corporate and I was just out here chasing wrecks, but I had my wife and my business to maintain, and I wasn't about to let a pretty pussy fuck up everything I had worked so hard to obtain. Yeah, I was smarter than the average bear, and I was about to show both ladies how the game was really played.

When I got home and saw how Shay had laid everything out I knew I had to go in double time with the work. Both of us had been extra busy, and neglecting each other, so it was time I showed my love some real attention. After I slammed dinner, I slam-dunked her ass right on the dining room table. I had her in there screaming and scratching at me like she was a virgin on top of the hood of my car. I tore that thing up like I did the very first night we were together, and when we got done I sent her up to the room to get ready for round two. An all-night beat session was about to transpire, and it was time to stake claim in what was mine again.

While she was upstairs getting ready I was downstairs tearing the place up looking for my phone. I knew I had left it home, but where was the question. I also knew Michelle had to have been blowing my phone up since I had brushed her off earlier in the day. I never missed a lunch date, and I could only imagine the kinds of messages she had left. I knew I couldn't take too long because she would come back down wondering why I wasn't up there. I quickly straightened up the kitchen and made my way up, hoping like hell that just maybe she didn't actually have the phone and I could find it before she did.

When I got upstairs Shay was laid out in nothing but glowing skin looking sexy as hell. I climbed into the bed, making a mental note to double back over the house, and look for the phone tomorrow while she was at work. Besides the fact that we barely had sex, Shay was the dream wife. Our home was maintained, and she handled her business well. Although I wasn't quite ready, I also knew that Shay would make a great mom. She wasn't putting any pressure on me, but I knew that having a baby would bring us back full circle. I just had to get the other factors out of the way before the issue became bigger than I could handle.

I didn't really believe her when I asked her about the phone. No, she didn't miss a beat when I inquired about it, but Shay was slick. Even if she had found it she wouldn't say anything right away. She would sit on the information until she could capitalize from it. That's how she worked. Which meant I would have to stay on my game until I either found the phone or she came clean with what she knew. That meant cutting off Michelle for a while, and that in itself would be another boiling pot on the stove that would bubble over if I didn't watch it carefully.

So let the games begin. I went upstairs and wore her ass out, putting her right to sleep. I wore myself out too, so my plans to get up and check her drawers while she was out were out of the question. I knew she had that phone somewhere, and it would surface sooner or later. I wasn't about to start stressing about it because that would just bring more attention to a situation that wasn't that serious. I would be ready or as ready as I could be when the time came. That's all I could do for now.

When we woke up the next morning I still couldn't get a good look in because Shay was on my heels. Like I said, I wasn't worried. It was going to be what it was going to be, and there was really nothing I could do to change the outcome at this point. I figured as long as I kept both of them at a low simmer I would be cool. That mode of thinking would come back to bite me later on, but I was prepared for what I had to deal with now. That was until I got to the shop.

When I pulled up I noticed a car out front that looked like Michelle's but I wasn't sure. It was still early, and she should have been at work. What would she be doing here? When I walked in I saw a curvy woman with her back to the door demanding to know where I was. I wanted to back out, but the bell chimed and she turned right around to stare me in my face. I was caught, and couldn't run if I wanted to.

She gave me the nastiest look when we made eye contact. I didn't think such a pretty face could look so mean. I quickly recovered, giving her the mean mug right back as I made my way into the shop. She was on my turf now, and I ran shit around these parts. It was time she recognized who was in charge.

"Was everything okay with your car, Mrs. Drayton?" I asked as I circled around the desk, standing next to my assistant. She looked so flustered in the face that I knew Michelle had to have been going in on her for a while.

"I've been to two other locations looking for you, Mr. Michaels. I need to discuss my car in your office."

"Sure, no problem," I said to her, pointing my finger toward the back of the store. "Hold any calls for me until I'm done with this situation," I told my assistant, ushering her to my office door. Once inside she took the liberty of locking the door. I took a seat behind my desk, and she walked around the other side instead of using one of the chairs in front of it.

"If there's nothing wrong with your car, what else can I help you with?" I asked her like I didn't know why she was there.

"Did you really think that you could just not show up? You already know what time lunch is served, Mr. Michaels, and you left me starving yesterday."

"Didn't I tell you a few days before that we were going to have to fall back for a while? My wife may be on to us, so I need to make sure things are straight there first before I continue things with you."

"Didn't I tell you I would give you a few days to figure it out?" she countered, stepping closer to me to stand in between my legs. She had me nervous for a second.

"Well I need more than a few days, Michelle. Maybe you should take more time to work on your situation as well," I threw back at her, trying to gain control of the situation. She was so close to me I could smell how sweet her pussy was, and was starting to salivate.

"Do you really want to stay away from all of this?"

She pushed my papers to the side and climbed up on my desk, spreading her legs wide. The little bit of light that came in from a crack in the blinds on the side window reflected light off of the jeweled clit ring she had. She was clean shaven and wet as fuck . . . I rocked up immediately.

She stroked her clit and tugged on her piercing a little to really get her juices flowing. She moaned softly, and I really hoped that she kept it low because my workers were bound to start showing up, and my assistant wasn't that far away. When she dipped her fingers into her juicy hole, and brought them back up to smear it on her clit I knew that there was no way I could let her leave without getting a little bit of her sweetness. That wouldn't be right at all.

I pulled my chair in front of her and leaned forward, capturing her clit on my mouth. If I'd known I would be having pussy for breakfast today I would have been better prepared. She tasted sweeter than I remembered, and when I stuck my tongue into her hole I had to catch myself from moaning out loud. Her walls clamped around my stiff tongue, and I couldn't wait to feel that same action around my dick. She had excellent control of her tight walls, and I knew that she knew she had me back open.

"Did you really think you could stay away from this?" she taunted me as I stood up to slide inside of her. I didn't even care that I didn't have a condom. I dropped my clothes to my ankles and went to work, tearing her ass up on the edge of the desk. I had to cover her mouth with my hand because this simple bitch was starting to get loud, and I could hear people stirring up out there. I didn't need anyone knowing this bullshit was even happening.

I gave her exactly what she wanted. An orgasm that shook her ass to the core. She looked like she was having a seizure for a moment as I snatched out and busted all over the front of her designer dress. There was no way I was busting inside of her with a wall up, and I just hoped none of my little guys snuck out in the process. At any rate, I pulled my clothes back up while she lay stretched out on my desk and I took my seat back in my chair looking very bored with the situation. It took her a few more minutes to get right, but she finally sat up looking down at the mess that I made on her dress.

"So, like I said. I will contact you when I can see you again. I need to get my home in order first. Understood?"

"I'll send you the bill for my dress," she replied as she wiped off what she could, then stood up to leave. She didn't even acknowledge what I said to her, and I knew at that moment that she was going to be more trouble than I could handle. Hopefully she would stay at bay and let me do what I need to do, but knowing Michelle that wasn't going to be the way it all went down.

Once she was gone, I sprayed my office with this Pink Sands spray that my wife got me from the Yankee Candle shop in Limerick to get the scent of sex out of the air. I was irked because I never had sex in my office, and the first time I did it wasn't with my wife. Not that Shay would do anything like that in the first place. Maybe if she did do little impromptu visits like that things would be better between us.

Washing Michelle off of me in the bathroom took a little longer because every time I thought about what just happened I would brick up again and I couldn't go out front on rock like that. Michelle was playing dirty, and the best way to get her back was to disappear. I called up the manager to at my Center City location to talk to him about splitting time between stores. I had to do a Houdini on this chick and disappear off the face of the earth for a while. I would just have to figure out what to tell Shay at a later date.

He agreed to handle both stores for me, and I informed my secretary that I wouldn't be in and to block me out on the calendar for two weeks. She ran the place perfectly so I wasn't worried, and she knew how to get in contact with me if it was necessary. As I drove back home I watched my rearview to make sure I wasn't being followed. Michelle definitely had a stalker's personality, so I had to be extra careful with her. I knew Shay would already be gone when I got home, so I would call her to let her know I had gone back home. I would just tell her I was feeling sick or something like that. At any rate, it looked like things were about to get complicated, and I needed to be ahead of the game so that I could look back to see what was coming.

28

Shay

Since Justin didn't know where his phone was I decided to grab it and hold on to it for a few days. While he cleaned up the table from dinner, I ran upstairs to turn the phone off and hide it in my top drawer so that I could look at it in the morning. It was like the alarm was on full blast the entire night because I didn't want him to know I had it. I had to refrain from getting up during the night and placing the phone in plain sight for him. There was something else going on in that phone and I would be finding out exactly what it was soon enough.

I wore his ass out in the bed that night, and when he woke up in the morning for work his legs still felt like they were replaced with wet noodles. I milked his dick bone dry, so even if he wanted to go give old girl another round he wouldn't have the energy. I even fed him breakfast and made sure his travel mug was filled with piping-hot coffee for the road. I didn't need him falling asleep behind the wheel or anything like that.

As soon as he was gone I ran and grabbed the phone from its hiding place, and when I powered it back up the phone was ringing off the hook with messages from his mistress. It was a good thing I did turn the phone off last night because she sent at least nine text messages throughout the course of the night, and if he would have heard the phone he would have wanted to know why it was in my drawer. This was one smart chick though, because not one time did she leave a voice mail.

Ignoring the texts for now, I sat and played with his phone to see if there were any other little hidden folders in it. I remembered that from watching an episode of *Cold Case,* and the husband on there kept all of his pictures and things from his wife of his mistress in a separate folder. At first there didn't appear to be anything going on. I didn't really know how to work this phone, so it was a little awkward trying to get through all the functions, but patience is a virtue and before I knew it I had found a folder in his documents that had the same name: 1BDBTCH.

To my surprise when I clicked on the folder it asked for a password. Now, he didn't password protect his phone completely because that would have given me reason to believe that there was something going on, but his simple ass put a password on a folder because he didn't want me to see this stuff. I could steadily feel the ice forming around my heart as I tried to figure out the password.

He made the shit too easy after I punched in his birthday, and then quickly punched in mine to gain access. It worked and I was irked that he would use my day to remember some other bitch. Typical dumb dude shit. As I browsed the folder all I was seeing was a bunch of pussy shots with my husband's dick stuffed in it. I knew what my husband looked like, so I was sure that I was looking at him. There were like a million shots in all different positions, and it had to have been the same girl because all of the pussy pics looked the same. It also looked like the pics were taken over time because the sheets in the little bit of the bed I could see in the pictures changed colors sporadically. He had been hitting this chick for a while.

What pissed me off more was there was not one head shot of this bitch in the phone. Not in the text log, not in the folder, and not in his pics. All I saw was pictures of wrecked cars, and before and after shots of the ones that were fixed. I guess when they said pussy had no face that it was true because this bitch definitely didn't have one. At least not in his phone, and that just meant that I was going to have to take some extra measures to find out who she was. I decided to keep his phone at work in my desk so that he couldn't find it around the house. That way if I mistakenly left it somewhere he wouldn't know that I looked through it. I had to be smart about where I put his phone once I was done with it so that the situation wouldn't be flipped back on me.

By the time I got to work that day I was heated, but I knew who to call. A good friend of mine was a police officer, and actually worked with my neighbor up the block who killed her husband a few weeks ago. I knew that if I needed any information Sharla was the one to get the job done. All I had to do was run the digits and she was on it. I made my call to her the minute I got on my lunch break, and as soon as I got back from lunch I set up tracking on all three of Justin's phones. That way I would know exactly where he was in the city down to the exact address. I was going to find this chick, and they both were going to pay for trying to play me.

I promise you the only thing worse off than a cheating husband is the bitch he's cheating with being okay with holding the number two spot. Those were the worst kind because they would suck a man dry literally and figuratively. They were they "yes" bitches in the game, and would do whatever he said to keep him happy. Especially the shit that the wife would not do. What she didn't know was she was about to have him all to herself, but he would be coming with absolutely nothing to offer. *Let's see if she'll want his ass then.*

While out on my break after talking to Sharla, I noticed this guy trying to catch my eye at the bar. I was eating lunch at Shwank's Bar & Grill, and oftentimes there was a busy lunch crowd full of corporate America's finest. After brokering million-dollar deals all day, we all had to come out to get some nourishment at some point in the game.

At any rate, Mr. Friendly couldn't keep his eyes off me and it was almost uncomfortable. Every time I looked up from my salad and my iPad he was staring me down with a smile on his face. I returned the smile, but didn't bother to offer him the empty seat across from me. Although I was at lunch by myself, I did see a few of the higher-ups in the company dining and they all knew I was married. I didn't want to give them any reason to think that I was cheating on my husband, and I always kept it strictly professional. There was a morality clause that my company had in place to protect its image, which meant if you got caught cheating or making the company look bad you could consider yourself fired and sued. Nobody wanted that kind of drama.

When my waitress brought my bill over, she told me it was taken care of by Bar Stool Guy. When I looked up he raised his glass and saluted. I raised mine back, and prepared my briefcase so that I could go back to the office. When I went to stuff my receipt in my bag I noticed his number scribbled on the back of it. As I was leaving I went toward the bar to get a good look at him, and he was even more handsome up close. I mouthed the words "thank you" to him as I passed, and gave him a smile. He smiled back and continued his conversation with one of the VPs from the company, so I knew it was a good choice to be discreet.

When I got back to my office, after setting up the tracking for Justin's phone I took out the receipt and plugged his number into my phone. I wasn't going to play around this early in the plan, but he looked like he might be fun. I put his name as Christina, because he had his name as

Chris on the receipt. This way if my husband decided to look into my phone there wouldn't be anything strange in my call log.

Things were coming together better than I thought, but I didn't want to get too cocky with it, so I stuck to the pace. I knew that to get my husband it would have to be direct and right in the face so that he wouldn't have room to lie. My mind did wander to Chris a few times, and I wondered what his voice sounded like. I just hoped to God that he didn't have a voice as light as mine. There is nothing sexy about a man of stature with a soft voice. Can you say *turn-off*? I was tempted to make the call but I didn't want to seem desperate so I decided to give it a few days.

Last night was serious, came the text from my husband. He must have been really thinking about me because rarely did I get a text from him during the day anymore unless it was something of importance.

Was it? I typed back, knowing that I had really put it down on him last night.

Yeah, it was. I'm still tired, and can hardly move my legs. What you trying to do to me?

I laughed out loud as I read the message. I started to tell him it was a setup, but he probably wouldn't get the joke. What I was hoping was that he would appreciate what he had, but men are greedy by nature so that conversation was a waste of time.

I'm doing what a WIFE is supposed to do. Hope you find time to take a nap. Tonight it's back on . . .

He simply sent a smiley face as a reply. I hated that Justin could bring out the worst in me, but he was out doing shit he had no business doing. I was going to wait a few days to check on the tracking to see where he'd been.

For his sake it all better be work related. A beast was ready to strike, and it was going to suck for him once it was out.

29

Justin

I texted my wife to see where her head was at. She still hadn't let on that she had my phone, but I wasn't about to press the issue. I was going to tell her that I was taking off the next two weeks, but I would just let her know once she came home later in the day. There was no need to stir the pot if it wasn't time yet. I had to handle Shay delicately because she would fly right off the handle, and it was hard to bring her back in sometimes.

I started looking for my phone in the most obvious place: my wife's dresser drawers. That's where most women put stuff of importance and stuff that they were trying to hide. I started from the bottom because that was where she probably thought I would look last. I was trying to see things the way my wife would, and I hoped that the phone would turn up. Ten minutes later I didn't find a phone, so next I checked the drawer in her nightstand.

When I opened it up I was not prepared for the number and sizes of dildos and vibrators that were packed inside of it. She had shit that I didn't have a clue how to use, and all kinds of lubes and gels to go with it. Why she never broke out any of this stuff when I was home was a mystery to me. When did she use this stuff, and with who? I could already see my mind was starting to wander, so I just slammed the drawer shut before I called her back. I didn't want to think about no man doing to my wife what I was doing to

Michelle, and all the other wives I'd slayed over the years. I bet if Michelle's husband knew what she was doing to me he would have killed both our asses on sight.

After looking under the bed and through the dirty clothes, I went downstairs to search the couches. The phone had to be in the house unless it fell out in one of the trucks, but I thought for sure that I had all of them when I left for work the other day. I wasn't about to ask her again because I didn't want her to start getting suspicious, but they were phones I used for work so I was sure she could understand the importance of having it.

I tore through the house like a hurricane, and then was mad I had to put it all back together when I was done. The phone was missing in action for real, so I figured I would ask Shay to put a track on it when she got home. Maybe I could find it that way. Either way I just needed it back. I had contacts in that phone for business, and I wasn't sure if the store could transfer my phone list somehow. If push came to shove I would just buy another one, but I needed that one back.

Once the house was straightened up I decided I would surprise my wife by cooking her dinner. It had been awhile since I had done anything like that for her, and it might just help bring us closer. I was willing to at least give it a try because on some real shit Michelle had me a little nervous, and I really didn't want to have to deal with her if I could get away with it.

30

Shay

"Mrs. Michaels, I would like you to meet Christopher Paige. He will be working with you on the McKesson Project. Catch him up to speed so that he can pilot you from here on out."

Imagine my surprise when my boss brought in the guy from the bar and grill yesterday. I wondered if he knew he was going to work with me, and that was why he paid for my lunch. But he did include his number so I didn't know. He had to know about the morality clause when he got hired, so there was no way he was dumb enough to write his number down in front of the VP. Or maybe he did it while he wasn't looking. Either way, he was a major distraction. One that I was not ready for.

"Nice seeing you again," Christopher said as he took a seat in one of the chairs in front of my desk. I was hoping that he wasn't one of those guys who had an extra-soft voice, and he wasn't. He wasn't Barry White deep with it, but it had a nice bass that made you pay attention when he talked. It made me tingle a little on the inside.

"Likewise." I smiled at him, getting caught up in his smile again. "So, let's take a look at your accounts and you can tell me what you already know."

He took the liberty of moving his chair around to the side of my desk, placing his laptop next to mine so that we could clearly view and share files. He smelled delicious, and his cologne swarmed around me like a warm breeze, making me feel a little dizzy.

"So, the McKesson accounts work like this . . ."

We spent most of the morning going over the ins and outs of the project, and what our role was on the committee. We got through a lot of the files, transferring money to where it was supposed to be, and building profit margins to match. I found Christopher easy to work with, and before we knew it we had a flow going that made getting through the project a lot less tedious.

"So that's pretty much what we have to do for the project," I said to him as the clock reached noon. Just as I was bending over my stomach made the most embarrassing noise ever. Can you say mortified? The look on my face said it all, and I was almost uncomfortable to even look his way.

"It's okay, I'm hungry as well. Why don't we let our brains rest for a while and grab a bite to eat?"

"Yes, let's," I said, relieved that he made light of the situation. We gathered our stuff up, and made our way out the building.

Over lunch we had a lively conversation, and I learned a lot about Christopher. He was a Harvard Business grad, and surprisingly still single. When I inquired why he was single he simply said, "It's easier that way."

I totally understood that shit. Marriage was hard work, and even harder when you find out you can't trust the person you've grown to love. It was a heartbreaking moment, one that silenced me for a brief moment. Did I want to make my relationship work or did I want him to pay?

"Well, it looks like we should get back to work. Lunch on me, okay?" he said as he set his card down to cover the bill.

"Okay, but next time it's on me."

"Or you can pay for dinner."

I ignored his last statement as I gathered my stuff up. He was flirting, but I wasn't about to fall in line that easily. We worked together, and I didn't need shit to be weird between us. He had to know that we could both get fired if we got caught. Walking ahead of him, I kept my face straight because I knew he was watching me walk. Christopher had already drawn the line with his indecent proposal; I just had to decide if I was going to take him up on that offer.

Once we were back in the office he kept it strictly professional and I was grateful for that. I didn't need him trying to finger my pussy under the desk while we were trying to work. By the end of the day we had gotten a lot accomplished, and our boss came into congratulate us on a job well done thus far. I was nervous about being partnered up, but he turned out to be an asset.

"Call me so that we can go over some things later tonight," he said to me as we were gathering our stuff to leave. I told him okay, but I had no plans to call him at all if I could help it. There was something magnetic about him that scared me a little, and although I knew he was going to be trouble, I almost wanted it.

Before I left the office I decided to see if my tracking software was even worth the trouble. I typed in the phone numbers I had for my husband, and two phone locations actually still read to be at my home address, which meant that my husband was already home. The third phone came up as being at my job address. What was he doing home was the big question. Men can never stay on track too long, so I knew if this was indeed a slipup he would do it again.

31

Justin

By the time she got home dinner was made, and the house was spotless. I could see the surprise on her face, and surprisingly it made me happy as well. Shay and I used to genuinely have a good time together, and it was time we got back on the right path. I took her briefcase and her jacket from her, resting them on the chair in the living room. When she sat down on the couch I took her shoes off, and rubbed her feet. She lay back on the couch and looked at me with a puzzled but pleased look on her face as I catered to her.

My foot massage inched up to her ankles and her calves as I tried to rub the day away. She didn't have on any stockings, so I could see that she had on a thong from the way her legs were positioned. She gave me a challenging look like she was daring me to make a move, and so I did. I pulled her down so that she could lie flat. Pushing her skirt up over her hips, I wished for a second I had kept her shoes on her feet as I pulled her thong to the side and tasted her. Heels were sexy as hell to me, and even better when that was all she had on. That turned me on even more, and I rushed to get to the treasure even faster. I was surprised that she actually tasted like she just washed up, and not like she had been out all day. I mean, I wasn't expecting it to be nasty, but I was expecting a little sweat at least. Why would she wash up before coming home?

She didn't appear to be caught off-guard by anything, and might just have been letting me know that she was out there, too. I hoped for her sake that maybe she had stopped off to the gym or something, and that was why she showered, because whoever she was seeing was going to be in for a rude awakening by the time I was done with them.

I topped her off lovely, and drilled into her right on the couch, not even bothering to use the rhythm method like we discussed. If she thought for one second she was going to leave me for some other dude she would be taking a baby with her. Damn all that noise. I was so mad, and I pounded the pussy like I was mad at it. She was steadily begging me to either stop or slow down, and that just made me do it harder and faster. Before I knew it I had taken hold of her throat and was pressing down on her neck.

"Whoever he is you better end it," I threatened her as I pounded into her. I was totally in a zone, and when I looked down again she was choking and her face was wet with tears. That shit scared the hell out of me. Did I almost kill her? She somehow was able to push me back off of her to catch her breath, and I instantly felt like shit.

"Get off of me!" she managed to scream out as she pounded on my chest. Her face was soaked, and I could see the beginnings of a bruise around her neck where my hands were.

"Shay, I'm sorry. I don't know what came over me," I apologized as I stuffed my still-erect penis into my pants. *I can't believe I zoned out like that.* I was still irked that she was possibly cheating, but was now the time to bring it up?

"Get away from! Leave me alone!" she screamed as she jumped from the couch and ran upstairs.

I didn't even bother to chase after her because I was dead wrong. I didn't know how long I should wait it out because every time I neared the bedroom I could hear her still in tears. Maybe I took things too far this time. *Should I tell her what I was thinking?* I decided to go in there and just play it all out. This was a no-win situation anyway, so at the very least I'd get to tell her my side of the story.

"Shay, I'm sorry I hurt you," I began as I sat on the edge of the bed. She was wrapped up in her bathrobe, looking like she could kill me. Her eyes were swollen from crying, and her neck was bright red where my hands where.

"What is wrong with you, Justin? That shit was like you were raping me," she said as the tears began again. That made me feel even worse, but I had to at least explain myself.

"That wasn't my intention, Shay. You have to believe me. It's just that you've been acting real shady lately—"

"I've been acting shady? You're the one who's never home!" she cut me off. Nothing was coming out the way I meant it, and I was digging a bigger hole for myself by the minute.

"I'm working, Shay."

"More like gathering up more hoes."

"I'm not the one walking in here shower fresh after being at work all day."

"But you are the one . . . never mind. Just go ahead, Justin. I have a headache and I just want some quiet right now."

"No, say what you need to say. I'm the one who's what, Shay?" I asked her, hoping she would just say that she had my phone. Hell, we both knew that she had it, and that was why she was acting the way she was toward me. I wasn't about to throw myself under the bus though, so damn just coming out and saying it.

"You're the one who's doing whatever it is you're doing. I'm going to sleep. This conversation is over."

"We're not done talking—"

"Yeah, we are, and I really hope I don't have to say it again."

With that, she rolled over and turned her back to me. I was beyond irked, but I couldn't really be mad at her because I had nothing on her but a clean pussy. She could have been doing that for me as a surprise like she did with dinner the other day. Of course I had to come and fuck up everything, and now I would have to make it all up to her.

Leaving the room, I decide to bunk out in the guest room because it was going to be a cold, lonely night either way. As I lay there in the dark I had to wonder how in hell I got caught up in all of this shit in the first place. If it weren't for bad luck I would probably have had no luck at all. I was wrong for choking her out, I'd admit that, but I wasn't crazy enough to think that I was the only one doing wrong in this relationship. Women were slick and it would take some fancy thinking to figure out what Shay was up to, but that's exactly what I was about to do. She had dirt on me, but we were about to have dirt on each other because I wasn't about to be thrown under the bus by myself at the end of this. We were both going down in flames if I could help it.

32

Shay

I almost got caught up. What the hell made me think that Justin wouldn't notice that I had cleaned up? I had to. When Christopher and I left the office we had a nice conversation on the way down. As I made my way to the parking garage I noticed that he was looking up the street like he was waiting for the bus.

"Are you on SEPTA?" I asked him as I fished around for my car keys.

"Actually I am. I don't live that far from here so it's a lot easier to hop a cab or bus ride than to try to find parking every day. Some days I even walk down if it's nice. My condo is right in Old City," he explained, looking at me all intense like he had been doing all day.

"Well, I have to go that way to get on the expressway. I can give you a ride," I offered, hoping that my pussy cooperated long enough to let him out of the car. I never got involved with anyone in my company, and trust that there had been plenty of offers over the years. It just wasn't professional, and I was a once happily married woman. I didn't want to earn a reputation of having slept my way to the top. Not after having worked so hard to get my master's degree to get here.

"Are you sure? I don't want to inconvenience you," he replied, flashing that smile that made me weak again.

"It's no problem. My car is parked this way."

"Okay, well at least let me carry your briefcase. Wouldn't want to mess up that diamond manicure."

We laughed, and I passed my briefcase over, walking a little bit ahead of him, knowing he was enjoying the view. When we got to my car he made sure to open my door for me first, something that my husband hadn't done since our third date. Most times Justin was in the car way before I was. Once I was securely in he set both of our briefcases in the back seat, and then he got in, securing himself into the seat.

"Show me the way," I said to him as I pulled out. We still held conversation as he pointed me in the right direction, and I had to admit that I loved talking to him. He made it so easy to open up, and even once we got to his place we sat out front and talked for a good while. I found out a lot about Christopher the human, and not just the working professional who I was working on a project with. I actually liked him in a friend type way.

"So when I decided to move here I figured I would just step out on faith and take some chances. Especially since all of the others things that I had planned for never worked out. This was the first thing I walked into blindly and I've been on top ever since."

"Wow, I am very impressed with your courage. I don't think I would have been able to pull it off. I need a more solid foundation before I make any moves," I admitted to him. There was no way I was stepping out of anything on a wing and a prayer and hoping that it would go right. I needed everything to be sound and on point.

"You're a smart woman. You should give it a try sometime," he said, looking me in the eye again. "Want to come in? Let me show you what I've done with the place."

"I don't think I should. My husband is expecting me to be home soon," I said to get out of giving in. Justin was probably still out whoring around, and I beat him home most days. Even though the trace said that he was home, that really only meant that the phone was there. He could have easily left it in the house and went on without it. I just knew that I shouldn't be in this man's personal space like this, and if I went in there I wouldn't be able to say no to his advances.

"Oh, it will just take a minute. I'm really proud of my decorating skills. I'd like to think I am a designer of sorts." He laughed, but was serious at the same time. I thought about it for a second, and figured what harm would it be to just go take a quick look? *I might even get an idea for redecorating my own spot.*

"Okay, let's go, but I have to make it quick."

We hopped out of the car, and after he grabbed his briefcase we made our way up to his space. I didn't know what I was expecting, but I was not expecting it to be laid the way it was. The place was breathtaking. It looked like it was taken from pages of home decorating magazines with a twist of his own style added to it. It was very masculine, yet soft enough for a female to find her own place in the midst of things. Needless to say, I was very impressed.

"Your place is beautiful." I gushed like I'd never been in surroundings as fly as this. My own home was the truth as well, but this was just sexy.

"Thank you very much. My sister helped me with most of it, and a lot of the art is original pieces from her studio."

"Your sister paints?"

"My sister creates masterpieces," he bragged, sounding like a proud brother. "She teaches art at the School of Design in Boston, and she begged to create canvases for this space when we first came to look at it. She actually was the one who convinced me to get it because I was actually going to pass on it. Now that it's all done I'm glad I didn't miss out on it."

"It's stunning. Both of you did a great job."

As we walked from room to room, I was even more impressed the more I saw of his place. It made me want to go home and start a home improvement project to revamp my place. I squashed that idea almost immediately because I knew Justin's cheap ass would not even go for it. Not after all the money he spent getting custom-made this and that installed just the way I liked it.

"Can I offer you a drink?" he asked flirtatiously. I knew I should go, but he had me drawn in.

"No, I don't drink and drive."

"Well, what else can I offer you?" he asked seductively as he backed me into the island that sat in the middle of his kitchen. This man was too close for comfort, but I couldn't get up the strength to get him to back off. It was like I wanted him in my space, and I didn't know how I felt about that. Out of all the years I was married I never entertained the idea of letting anyone in. I was married, and once Justin and I tied the knot I was officially off the market. If I had to cheat I might as well be single.

None of that logic came into play as he lifted me on to the counter, and began to rub my body down. First the suit jacket, and then the pencil skirt . . . Pretty soon I was perched up on his counter in my birthday suit and my body was tingling all over. I was pulsating, and I wanted him to invade my body so bad. It scared me, and excited me at the same time. What was this man doing to me?

He parted my legs and pulled me to the edge so that I hung off the edge a little. He pulled up a stool, and took a seat right between my legs. I felt like a teenager sneaking to make out behind the bleachers, but I wasn't shy at all. I felt bold, and I wanted him to take me.

He rested one leg on each shoulder, and pressed my thighs open to spread me wider. His fingers felt warm as he parted my lower lips and stuck is tongue inside of me.

Electricity shot through my body, and I began to convulse as he slurped up my clit and sucked on my lips. He was giving me a sloppy head job, and I couldn't stop my lower half from grinding into his face. This shit felt so damn good, and when I gathered up my breasts and stuck my nipples into my mouth it shot me right to the next level. It had been way too long since I felt like this, and I almost felt bad for it.

I grabbed a hold of the edge of the counter as my body really began to shake uncontrollably, and the first orgasm I'd had in months came roaring through my body at the speed of a train, and I screamed and howled so loud I know the neighbors around the corner heard me. He locked my legs down and didn't let me go until every last drop was released and I was laid out on the counter damn near in a coma. This man had me open, and I wanted more.

"You okay up there?" he asked as he rose from between my legs, wiping his mouth on a paper towel.

"I think so," I managed to moan out, feeling guilty as hell all of a sudden. I never cheated on my husband before. That alone wasn't even why I felt guilty. I knew after this time I would want it again, and I just hoped that I could stay away.

"There's a linen closet in the bathroom. Go ahead and get yourself cleaned up. I don't want to hold you up more than I have."

I wanted to protest, but I knew he was right. When I was able to focus on the clock I saw that I should have been home a half hour ago. Even with that information I didn't even rush to the bathroom, and contemplated taking a ride on that hard-on that was having a hard time disguising itself in his slacks. Still, I knew I should leave, so I washed up quickly, dressed, and made my way to the door.

"I'll see you at the office bright and early, Mrs. Michaels. Be sure to get home safe and have a great night."

"You do the same," I threw over my shoulder as I raced down to my car, and across the city. I was expecting Justin to already be home when I got there, and when I got in the house I had no choice but to give him some too if he wanted it. A wife has to still handle her business at home regardless of what we did in the street. I didn't think it would turn into all that it did, but I knew I had to stay two steps ahead of Justin so that I wouldn't get caught up. I just hoped Christopher would make it easy to stay focused.

33

Justin

The next day was extra awkward, and it had me rethinking my idea of taking a vacation. *I'd rather deal with Michelle's bullshit than Shay's.* I didn't have to sleep next to Michelle every night, and on some real shit it was just a matter of cutting her off so dealing with her wasn't that deep. Now, Shay on the other hand was going to be a handful; she just didn't know how to let shit die, and could drag something out for weeks. I was so not in the mood for that, but what do you do when you feel betrayed also?

I got up a little earlier than her and made breakfast, and she walked right by that shit like there wasn't a scrambled egg or a slice of bacon on the table. Shay loved bacon, so that definitely solidified that we were at war. I tried to avoid this, but this was exactly what I got. I was going to figure it out though. Hell, marriages went through stuff and this was just another hurdle we had to cross to get back to being how we were.

After she left the house, I enjoyed breakfast since I took all that time to make it. I forgot to ask Shay to set up the tracking for my phones, and since she was mad right now I decided to just do it myself. I was hoping that the phone hadn't died yet so that the tracking could pick up a signal for it. It had to be in the house. When I logged into the account I was surprised to see that tracking was already set up for all three phones. When was she going to clue me in on that piece of information? So Shay was watching me at least for the last few days. Which meant that she had found the phone and was hiding it from me. When I looked at the tracking record it showed that she had taken the phone to work, but it didn't say that she had returned it to the house. She either had the phone turned off at the moment or the battery died. The fact that she lied to my face when I asked her about it was typical Shay bullshit that I saw through anyway. So since she wanted to roll like that, then it was time for me to join into the fun and games as well.

Instead of setting her phone up for tracking on our joint account, I created an additional account through Sprint where I could do the same things as her, but it was under an account that I created. Since she saw fit to check up on me I would return the same courtesy to her. It was a shame that it had come to this in our marriage, but that was how things were at this point, and hopefully it didn't bite both of us in the ass.

Checking the two phones that I still had I decided to leave them home, and go replace the phone that Shay had in her possession. That way I could still get any text messages and calls that I was missing right now. I wondered if Shay had found the file that I had stored with pictures of Michelle in it. I purposely moved those photos from plain view so that she couldn't see them. The file was password protected, and I made the password so easy it would be impossible to figure out.

When I got to the Sprint store I was irked that a new phone would cost me $300, but I had just gotten that phone and I didn't want to start a new line. As soon as I turned the phone on it was popping with texts back to back. I guessed since that other phone was powered down this phone was able to pick up all the messages that I had been missing.

Michelle was pissed with me. She sent the majority of the text messages that came through, and I could tell that she was getting tired of waiting for me. Her texts were borderline threatening, and I knew if I didn't call her soon she would start stalking me again. It had only been a day or so since I fucked her in my office, but Michelle really thought she belonged to me.

I tried to ignore her calls for as long as I could, but even after my nap I couldn't control my erection because I kept thinking about her. Michelle was a beast in her own right, and definitely gave Shay a run for her man. I mean, Shay was equally as freaky, but Michelle was just so nasty with her shit and she didn't care what it was that had to be done. I wished my wife could be more like that.

Before I knew it I was dialing Michelle up to see if I could get a lunch date. She answered immediately and agreed that we should meet up at her condo. Her husband was out of town for a few days so she was sure that I wouldn't have to worry about him coming in on us.

Where are you staying? I texted her to get an address. I pretty much knew the entire city, so I wasn't worried about trying to find it.

We have a condo right in Old City. Here is the address, she texted me back, giving me the house number and street name.

I got myself dressed and ready, leaving all of the work phones home except for the one I just replaced, and I took my personal phone in case Shay called. When I got to the condo, it realized that it wasn't too far from my wife's job and thought about stopping by once I was done with Michelle to give her some flowers. Or maybe I would see if she could sneak out for a late lunch, and I could take her to that little bar and grill that she liked across from the building she worked in.

When I got up to Michelle's condo I was not surprised that she answered the door asshole naked, except for the five-inch red pumps on her feet. Her body was everything, and I loved looking at it. She welcomed me in with a huge smile on her face, and by the time she got me stripped down to my skin and had me straddled I forgot all about the stress my wife was taking me through. There was no way I was going to be able to live in Philadelphia and not hit Michelle on a regular basis. I would just have to find a way to make it work. Even if it killed me.

34

Shay

Have you ever had a connection with someone that was so deep you couldn't even think straight? I'm talking about the kind that had you so far gone you didn't know how to find your way back, and you really didn't care if you ever did? That's the kind of situation that I had building up with Christopher. So much so that I totally forgot about keeping tabs on my own man because I was too busy sniffing around behind him. He had me open with a capital O, and I didn't care who saw it. Fuck that morality clause that I signed when I got hired. I was going to give Christopher as much of me as he wanted, and I didn't care who knew.

It was almost impossible to stay strictly professional at work. Christopher remained about his business, but on lunch breaks I would sometimes close my office door so that we could let our hair down a little. The things he did to me in that corner office had to be considered a sin, and since I was probably on my way to hell for this anyway I might as well enjoy the ride. Christopher did shit to me, and took me to heights that I thought were unobtainable. Both in the bedroom and in work ethic. He brought a view to each project that we talked that made everything make much more sense than it had previously. We were the dream team, and even the higher-ups noticed the high standard of work we put in to make the company more money.

Christopher had more than my body; he had my mind, and there were times when I had to catch myself around him because I thought for sure I was falling in love. I needed him. I feigned for him, and at the times that he was not around I spent all of that time counting the minutes that we would be back together. He wanted me. I wanted him. We wanted each other, but I had Justin. That fucking sucked.

Justin had changed too, and I could see that we were disconnected. In the mornings we barely said two words to each other, and by the time I got dressed for the day he had already left without even saying good-bye. He also stopped inquiring about that missing cell phone weeks ago, which meant he probably just replaced it with another. Truth be told I didn't even care anymore. I would have walked away from all of this shit right now to be with Christopher, but I wasn't stupid. We both had an image to uphold, and outside of mind-boggling sex what else did we really have?

Okay, so there were some feelings there. You can't share yourself with someone continuously without something developing. It was nearly impossible, but I had to admit that it was getting more difficult by the day to keep going home without him. My bed at home was cold, and most nights Justin slept in the guest bedroom. I didn't bother to protest or fake like I missed him in my bed because I didn't. Whoever he was seeing could have him full time, and if it was just that cut-and-dried he probably would have been rolled out.

He was afraid to leave because he thought I would take him for everything he had, and he was right. We had this conversation jokingly before we got married, but at this point I was willing to walk away with half, and he could have the house. I just needed to know how Christopher really felt before I made a move like that. He pushed me to throw caution to the wind, but I was always cautious about our situation. I wasn't sure if he was what I needed, but he was damn sure what I wanted.

The opportunity to really have Christopher all to myself without sneaking around came about a month later when we were selected to present a new product to our sister company in Texas. They would be sending us down there for two weeks to introduce the new McKesson system, and to get the company up and running so that we could all be on the same operating system. This way, when it came time to coordinate and share info files wouldn't have to be converted to do it. This was the day Christopher and I worked so hard for, and to see it come into fruition right in front of our eyes was reward within itself. This also meant a huge raise, and a nice bonus. I was ready to run full steam ahead with it.

The night I told Justin about the trip was uneventful. At first I was irked that he acted like he didn't care that I would be gone for a few weeks. It was like he had given up on our marriage already, but it was cheaper to keep me so he figured we could just work out as roommates. I mean, he didn't say it, but that's how it all came off.

"So, my job is sending me to Texas for two weeks to start up the McKesson project for our sister company. I'm excited that I even got picked," I said to him one night over dinner. We weren't even looking at each other, and I was doing most of the talking.

"Good for you. I'll be here when you get back. Make sure you bring me a souvenir," was his dumb-ass reply that made me want to throw my plate at him. A souvenir? Really? He could be such a dick sometimes, and this was definitely one of them.

I wanted to talk to him about a lot of shit, like where our relationship was going. We were barely spending any time together, and even when we did have sex it was forced and not enjoyable. There wasn't even any foreplay involved. He would just slide in from the side, fuck me hard until he came, and when he was done he would roll over and go to sleep. He didn't even bother to make sure I got one off like he normally did, and most times when he did grab for me I was half asleep. By the time I got in the swing of what was happening he was done, and asleep. Christopher would have never done that. On the nights we did share a bed this is how it went down every time.

I had also been starting to feel a little under the weather lately. He was already gone before me most mornings, so he didn't witness the bouts of sickness that had me crawling to the bathroom. I rose early in the morning just so I could get my head on straight enough to get to work on time. I was tired all the time, and couldn't keep anything down. Even Christopher noticed that I was a little under the weather, and would bring me broth and crackers since I couldn't tolerate anything else. I was convinced that maybe I had gotten a stomach bug due to the change in the weather. One minute it was cold as ice, and the next warm. You really didn't know how to dress most days.

It wasn't until a few days before the trip that I realized something else might be wrong. I was going through the closet in the bathroom before a quick store trip to make sure I didn't need to stock up on anything. When I peeked into my tampon box I realized that I had hardly used any, and I couldn't remember the last time I had even popped one in. Running out of the room, I grabbed my phone so that I could take a look at my calendar. I documented all important things in my phone so that I could keep the information right at my fingertips.

Scrolling back through the months I realized that my last recorded menstrual cycle was almost ten weeks ago, and I hadn't had one yet this month. Was I pregnant? I dismissed the idea quickly, chalking up my missing period to being stress related. Between the project and long hours at work, the bullshit going on in my home life, and trying to keep up with Christopher I was stretched way too thin, and I knew I needed to pull back from something or someone. I just couldn't decide which man it was going to be because both was not an option.

I caught myself pushing the thought out of my head, but the more I thought about it the more worried I got. It was Saturday. So my doctor's office was closed, and even if I called for an appointment on Monday, if it wasn't an emergency they probably wouldn't be able to see me for a few weeks. I was not going to be able to wait that long, so while I was in Walmart gathering toiletries I made sure to pick up an E.P.T. pregnancy test. I knew I couldn't take it home, so after I paid for everything I had I put my bags in the car, and doubled back to the store to pee on the stick. I needed to know now, and I needed to figure out what I was going to do if it came out positive.

Taking a seat in the stall, I followed the directions on the box, laying it flat down as I waited for the three minutes to pass on my watch. I didn't want to look at the results before then because I didn't want to freak out in here prematurely. Was this really what my life had resulted in? Taking pregnancy tests in store bathrooms? I felt so stupid and confused, and I knew that I needed to make a decision about what I was going to do with the two men in my life. Even if I wasn't ready, the results from this test would come with me having to make moves and choices whether I wanted to or not.

When the three minutes finally passed I got up the courage to look at the test, and sure enough two lines popped up, indicating that I was indeed pregnant. I sat down on the toilet and cried my heart out. What the heck had I done? I didn't know who to go to first because although I had been sleeping with Christopher more, my husband and I had managed to have sex a few times. I didn't know who this baby belonged to. Grabbing my phone I called Christopher up immediately. His reaction would determine how I broke the news to my husband.

"Why are you crying? What happened?" Christopher asked in concern once he detected my voice on the phone.

"I need to come there now. We need to talk," I sobbed into the phone. I was so disappointed that I even let myself get caught out here like this. How was I going to explain this to my husband?

"I'm at the house. You can come now. Just let me know when you are here, and I will buzz you in."

"Okay, I'm on my way."

I raced through the city in a daze and a ball of confusion not believing I got caught out there like this. I was too old to be making this kind of mistake. What would Christopher think of me once I told him what was going on. Would he look at me differently? Would he even still want to be involved? Just thinking about that made me feel sick on my stomach, and I had to pull over to the side of the road to vomit. I was not prepared for all of this, and I felt like I was walking into the lion's den. I had to prepare myself for possibly being rejected by him, and I knew I wasn't ready for that.

When I pulled up to his building I found a spot, and sat in my car a little while longer, hesitant to go upstairs to see him. We were supposed to be celebrating our achievement on the job, and here I went with baby momma drama. Gathering my pocketbook, I decided to just go and get it over with. Whatever the outcome was I would just have to deal with it.

35

Justin

"Did you really think you could stay away from this?" Michelle moaned in my ear as she squeezed the walls of her pussy around my dick. This girl had my toes curled, and my body was so rigid I thought I would pull a muscle if I didn't relax somehow.

"I . . . I had to teach you a lesson," I moaned back, knowing I was truly the one being schooled. She smirked at me in a way that let me know she knew that I knew she was in charge. Turning her body to the side, she got up on her feet and bounced up and down on me, the sound of her bare ass connecting with my skin was like music to my ears. She was so damn nasty it didn't make any sense, and I loved her for it.

It got serious in there. The headboard was banging up against the wall, and we practically flipped each other around the bed jockeying for the top position. I was sweating so hard I could barely see, and we were so slippery we couldn't even really get a grip on each other. I was up deep in her guts and it felt like my orgasm was building up from my toes. I wanted to scream, but I couldn't find my voice. I was trying to hold out until the last second, but I couldn't control myself anymore. It felt like every bit of semen I had in me came out at that moment and I collapsed on her in an exhausted heap.

"That must have been great. I haven't seen her perform like that in years," a male voice came from over my shoulder. Jumping up in shock, I came face to face with a man who couldn't have been anyone else but Michelle's husband. Here I was naked with his wife's juices on my dick, and he caught a glimpse of everything. What could I say at this point?

"What are you doing back here?" Michelle yelled from the bed as she too jumped to cover herself up. I grabbed a pillow from the bed to hide myself as he stood there and looked at us both. The crazy thing was he didn't even seem upset by what was happening. I on the other hand would have come in swinging. He merely gave us a smirk as he brushed invisible lint from his Armani suit.

"I came to surprise my wife with a night on the town since I hadn't really been giving you time, but it seems you have been filling your time . . . among other things . . . with your new friend here."

"Listen, I didn't know—"

"Oh, you knew. They all know. If you think you are the only man she is screwing you are not as bright as I want to give you credit for."

I looked from him to her in disbelief. If there were so many why was she stalking me so hard? This chick had me compromising my situation at home, and here it was she had me in a rotation. I was ready to choke her out, but I didn't know what old boy was going to do if I went after her.

"You see," he went on to explain, "my dear wife here is a horny little devil who will screw anything who's moving. I've never been enough for her and I know it, so that's why I allow her to do what she wants. I'm surprised that you stuck around for so long. Especially after her revealing that she has herpes."

My world began to swirl right before my eyes. *Did this man just tell me she has a disease?* I didn't use a condom the last few times Michelle and I had sex, and I had been having sex with my wife. Was he telling me that I could have possibly passed something to her?

It was like an out-of-body experience as I swung around and grabbed her by her neck and began punching the shit out of her. She could have possibly not just ruined my life but my wife's, too. I was going in, naked and all, and all I could hear was her screaming as she rolled up in a ball to try to get away from me. I didn't even know what the husband was doing all this time, but I halted instantly when I heard the first gunshot ring out.

"That's enough, young man," he spoke to me in a calm voice. "Now, I'm going to give you one minute, and not a second more, to get your stuff and get out of my house. I suspect that I won't see you around these parts anymore. You understand where I'm going with this, right?"

I didn't bother to answer. I simply jumped into my pants and I put my shoes on hurriedly, opting to finish getting dressed in my car. I could hear Michelle's sobs, and her constantly telling me that she was sorry. I didn't know what he had planned for her, and I couldn't care less. Now I had to figure out what the hell I was going to tell my wife when I got home. This was some bullshit, and a serious reminder why cheating was never worth it in the end. Grabbing my keys and my phone I ran out of her condo only to bump into my wife on the way down. Did she follow me here? I had to look extra crazy rushing out of the building half naked, and there was really nothing left but to tell the truth.

"We need to talk," I said to her as I turned her around to keep from entering the building. She looked like she had been crying, and she looked in disbelief. I was caught red-handed and there was no squirming out of it. I had to face the music and deal with the outcome whether I was ready to or not.

36

Shay

What the hell was Justin doing here? I was totally caught by surprise when he almost knocked me down running out of Christopher's building. And why didn't he have hardly any clothes on? Did he find out about Christopher and they got into a fight? I was scared to ask, and afraid to follow him home. This was too much happening too fast, but if I went into the building he would want to know why I was over this way. Instead of putting up a fight, I turned and went back to my car and went home. I didn't see his car when I pulled out so I assumed that he went on without me and I would just meet him there.

When I pulled up his car was in the driveway. I took my time going in because I still didn't know what to expect, and I didn't want to give up any information until I absolutely needed to. Hell this might just be a way out of the relationship, and then I could really just be with Christopher and we can go our separate ways.

"I know what you are thinking, and I can explain," he said in a rushed tone like he had gotten caught red-handed. I didn't say a word; I just took a seat across from him, and looked at him so that he could explain.

"I'm sorry that you had to follow me around, and trace my phone. I knew I had no business stepping out on you, and I'm sorry you had to find out that way."

I sat quiet, not saying a word, as I digested everything he said. Apparently he thought I followed him over there, and that I had been crying because I found out about his cheating. In reality I was there to battle my own demons, but I had no idea this thing would work in my favor.

"So how long have you been seeing her?" I asked him to gauge if we had been stepping out on each other the same amount of time. Not that it really mattered. At the end of the day we both were dead-ass wrong, and we should have handled our situation better.

"It's only been for a few months. I don't know an exact date, but I do know that I shouldn't have entertained her in the first place."

I remained quiet. There was no way I could possibly point fingers at him with the stress and the mess I was holding on to. I'd have been lucky if he didn't punch me in my face once I told him I was pregnant and it might not be his.

"Listen, I fucked up big time and I have to tell you something that you may not want to hear."

A zillion thoughts popped into my head at that moment. Was he about to break up with me? I was nervous because even though I kept saying that I didn't want him, now that it was actually a possibility I wasn't too sure if that was the way to go. I was always talking shit about how I didn't need him, but what if Christopher didn't want me? Did I really want to be by myself? This was too much to take in at one time, and it was giving me a headache.

"We may need to go get checked out. The woman I was cheating with had herpes, and I may have contracted it and passed it on to you."

Floored. *Did he just say that he possibly gave me an STD?* I was speechless for what felt like forever before I could even make a sound, and when I did it came out in an agonizing scream that I was sure could be heard for blocks. If he had indeed given me a disease how would I explain it to Christopher? I was so in shock and turmoil that I wanted to die on the spot. None of this was supposed to be this difficult, and it was just supposed to be something fun to do. Both of us got caught up majorly, and everything was just a mess now. He got down on the floor to hold me and I just cried and cried in his arms. He kept trying to assure me that everything was going to be okay, but I knew it wouldn't be. What I had to tell him was just as bad, if not worse, than what he just revealed to me.

"Shay, we can get through this. Trust me. We can go to the doctor in the morning to get it all figured out," he said as he tried to console me. I was distraught on so many levels and I couldn't take it anymore.

"Justin, I'm pregnant."

He stopped rocking me back and forth and froze. I was afraid to even make eye contact because that wasn't even as deep as it got.

"You're pregnant?" he asked me like he didn't just hear what I said. I hesitated, but I knew what I had to say next would change the game forever.

"Yes, I'm pregnant, and it might not be yours."

His face crumbled, and I could see the hurt in his eyes. I didn't want to care, but I did. I didn't hate Justin. We had history. We just somehow lost our way, and we both brought something home that we didn't want. He hung his head down to his chest soon I saw the tears fall. I wanted to comfort him but I didn't know how. My mind strayed for a second to Christopher, and I knew he must have called me a hundred times to find out why I hadn't gotten there yet, but I left my phone so that it wouldn't ring while I was talking to Justin. I knew I wouldn't be calling him back tonight though. It was just something I would have to deal with at work the next day.

Justin and I both got up from the floor, and I followed him up to the bedroom where we just lay, and held each other until we fell asleep. Our relationship was so off track, and I wasn't completely sure if we could put it back together or if we even wanted to. There was so much on the table right now, and so many issues that we had to deal with. There was a disease and a baby in question, and although we had been strong about things in the past this one might actually be a deal breaker.

I prayed that whatever the outcome was we could both deal with it because right now we were surely just trying to process what just happened. This was the kind of stuff that you hear about, but never think it would happen to you. Nothing good ever comes from cheating, and this was hopefully a lesson learned for both of us.

37

Conclusion

We managed to get through what was left of the week-end, and on Monday morning we were quiet as we both got dressed and prepared to go to the doctor. I was so nervous about so many things; Justin hadn't said a word to me since last night. He wasn't standoffish or treating me bad, but he was quiet and in thought. We both were. What if we had a disease? A baby I could get rid of, but herpes was the gift that kept on giving.

We drove in silence, taking his car instead of two. I called out from work against better judgment, but I assured my boss that I would be ready for the Texas trip and that I was just feeling a little under the weather. When I got to my phone the next morning I only had 3 percent battery life left, but it was enough to see that Christopher had called my phone over a hundred times, and he had also sent an abundance of text messages and even left voice mails. I knew I would have to reach out to him at some point during the day, but right now that wasn't top on the priority list.

When we got to the doctor I was extra embarrassed as I told him why we were there. Having to say out loud again and admit to my infidelity did something to me on the inside that felt damaging. Why did it even have to get to this point? Justin seemed to grow more and more distant as the minutes passed, and I felt so alone in all of this.

"So both of you may have contracted a sexually trans-
mitted disease, and you think you are pregnant?" the
doctor repeated to me as he scribbled in his chart.

"Yes, that's pretty much what's going on."

"Okay, I will do an exam on both of you today, and
we will get blood work done. With herpes, if the woman
in question wasn't in an outbreak period, you may have
dodged the bullet. Which of you will be examined first?"

"I will," I spoke up, wanting to get this humiliating
experience over with. It was so degrading and so uncalled
for. I was irked that we were even here for this prevent-
able shit.

The doctor stepped out of the room to give me time to
undress from the waist down. He also informed me that
he would be doing an ultrasound once the urine test was
confirmed that I was positive for pregnancy to see how
far I was. As I undressed and got up on the table I felt like
I was going to cry. Justin came to me and held my hand,
and I could see tears in his eyes also.

"Shay, I'm sorry for all of this and I really hope we can
figure it out. I had no business stepping out, and I feel like
I probably pushed you out there because of all the women
I dealt with. Whatever the outcome I'm willing to stay to
make it work."

I cried because I knew that at the end of all of this Justin
was where I was supposed to be. The doctor came back and
let me know that there were no visible signs of a herpes
outbreak, but the blood test would let him know for sure if
it was in my system. The ultrasound revealed that I was ten
weeks pregnant, and counting back there was a possibility
that it might belong to my husband. A penile swab and
blood tests were run on my husband as well, and we would
have to wait the week for the final test results.

When we left the doctor's office that day I decided
that I would cut Christopher off. I would let him know

I was pregnant because it was the only fair thing to do, but I would also let him know that I would be working things out with my husband and that it wasn't in our best interest to see him anymore. It was probably wrong of me, but I would not be mentioning the herpes situation until I got the results back. If I was clean there was no use in bringing it up.

Things were still tense with me and Justin for a while after the doctor's visit, and each day I could see the progress of us starting to gravitate back toward each other. I went on my trip to Texas for the company, and managed to stay in my hotel room without feeling the urge to dip down and see Christopher. I stayed on the phone with Justin every night until I fell asleep, and when he called to reveal that the test results were back and that we didn't have any diseases I was relieved. Now we could truly move forward in starting over.

By the time I got back home it felt weird, but I actually missed him while I was away and when we made love that night it was off the charts. This was an experience that truly grounded me, and I knew for certain that cheating wasn't for me. Luckily we were able to survive this horrible time in our lives, and when the baby was finally born the paternity test proved that it was Justin's child. That brought a joy to us that was unexplainable.

Thankfully, Christopher didn't give me too much grief, although on more than one occasion I caught him giving me the eye like he wanted to eat me alive. He was very understanding, and even got me the largest gift when my company gave me a baby shower. Christopher and I were on a very dangerous path that could have ruined both of our careers. He asked me what happened the day I was supposed to go talk to him, but respected the fact that I didn't want to go into detail. He simply gave me a hug, and wished me well with my marriage to Justin, and we kept moving forward. It was bittersweet but it had to be done.

Needless to say, this was a lesson for anyone who is not faithful. It's a dangerous game, and a happy ending isn't always the outcome. Justin and I lucked out, but there are many others out there who don't have luck on their side. Justin and I were finally on track, and even with hurdles we still worked it out. Lucky me . . . lesson learned!

Domestic Violence is a serious situation. If you or anyone you know is in an abusive situation there is help. Don't wait until it's too late!

Women don't have to live in fear:

In the US: call the National Domestic Violence Hotline at 1-800-799-7233 (SAFE).

UK: call Women's Aid at 1-808-200-0247.

Canada: call the National Domestic Violence Hotline at 1-800-363-9010.

Australia: call 1-800-RESPECT at 1-800-737-732.

Worldwide: visit International Directory of Domestic Violence Agencies for a global list of help lines and crisis centers.

Male victims of abuse can call:

US and Canada: the Domestic Abuse Helpline for Men & Women

UK: ManKind Initiative

Australia: One in Three Campaign

Notes